MW01045408

Shoot to Score

Sandra Richmond

James Lorimer & Company Ltd., Publishers
Toronto, 1998

© 1999 Sandra Richmond

First publication in the United States, 1999

James Lorimer & Company Ltd. acknowledges the support of the Department of Canadian Heritage and the Ontario Arts Council in the development of writing and publishing in Canada. We acknowledge the support of the Canada Council for the Arts for our publishing program.

Cover illustration: Sharif Tarabay

Canadian Cataloguing in Publication Data

Richmond, Sandra, 1948-
  Shoot to score

(Sports stories)
ISBN 1-55028-643-9 (bound)
ISBN 1-55028-642-0 (pbk.)

I. Title. II. Series: Sports stories (Toronto, Ont.).
PS 8585.I38S56 1998   jC813'.54   C98-932591-1
PZ7. R52Sh 1998

James Lorimer & Company Ltd., Publishers
35 Britain Street
Toronto, Ontario
M5A 1R7

Distributed in the United States by:
Orca Book Publishers,
P.O. Box 468
Custer, WA USA
98240-0468

Printed and bound in Canada.

Contents

To Jim and Mike:
Thank you for the joy
you have brought into my life.

1

A Tough Tryout

Steven leapt forward, his skates scraping the ice as he stick-handled the puck around the cones. It was hard to keep the puck under control and not to hit the bright orange markers. Josh was ahead by two cones but Steven just couldn't go any faster or he would lose control.

Josh sped past the last cone and, flying toward the goal, he drew back his stick and slapped the puck. It soared over the goalie's right shoulder and into the net.

Steven followed, shifting his stick quickly from one side of the puck to the other. As he neared the goal he smacked the puck through the air, just missing the top of the net. His heart sank as he felt the coaches watching him. Rats, Steven thought, I was sure I would get that one. Skating around the back of the net, he wondered if he'd caught a smirk on Josh's face.

* * *

Untying his skates after the final tryout, Steven was fully aware that the coach was posting his selection on the bulletin board. The guys gathered around, impatiently pushing, eager to see who had made the West Van peewee rep team. Steven took a deep breath and made his way toward the board. The change room was very warm and he could feel a row of sweat bubbles popping out across his forehead.

He wanted to be on the team so badly. This year the peewee rep team, along with the bantam rep team, was going to Colorado Springs for a tournament in February. Two years ago, when his brother Jeff was a peewee, Jeff had gone, scored six goals and come home the MVP. Jeff didn't have to worry about making the team, he always did, and their Dad was always proud of him. Steven didn't think he could stand it if Jeff got to go twice and he didn't get to go at all.

As Steven approached the board his best friend, Will, was right in front of him. He turned around, their eyes met, and Steven's heart stopped.

"It sucks," Will said angrily. With his wiry strength he kicked his bag before picking it up, slung it over his shoulder and slumped towards the change room door. An angry flush darkened his Nordic good looks.

Steven's throat went tight. If Will hadn't made the team, there wasn't much hope for him, he reasoned. He swallowed to hold back the tears and searched the list for his name. It was there. Right at the bottom of the *B* list. Steven Edwards, defence. He had tried out for defence because most of the guys wanted to play forward and he thought he'd have a better chance of making it. Nice *fat* chance, he thought angrily. Now not only am I not on the rep team but I have to play defence.

Steven remembered his father's words. He had meant them as encouragement but now they came back to him, sharp and painful. "The rep team is where you want to be. The level of hockey is more advanced. You play way more games and you get better coaches. Work for it, Steven. I know you can make it."

Steven's eyes travelled back up the list to see who else was on the *B* team. At least he and Will would be playing together, he comforted himself. Amar and Shogo were there from his team last year. He didn't know the others. Last year Claire Andrews had been on Steven's team but this year only guys had tried out. He knew there would be girls on some of the other teams and wondered why Claire had dropped out. The coach was Dan Carter, and Steven had heard he was mean and tough. His twin sons, Josh and Andrew, were also listed on the *B* team. Oh great, a family affair, Steven thought to himself. He and Will sat quietly on the curb outside the ice arena waiting to be picked up. It was part of a huge community complex in the centre of West Vancouver. Steven's disappointment made him feel heavy and numb. How was he going to tell his dad? What was he going to say to Jeff?

* * *

Steven was lying on the couch in the family room that was attached to the kitchen when Jeff came crashing in the back door. He slammed his school binder onto the kitchen table and yanked open the refrigerator, making everything shake. His blond curly hair was cut short, giving him a definite jock look. He grinned, loving the noise he was making. With his new deep voice he yelled at his brother.

"Hey, bro, Mr. Couch Potato, how about coming outside and smacking some pucks with me?"

"Naw." Steven's eyes never left the TV. He wanted to go out with Jeff but he knew he would ask about the tryout.

"Come on, ya wussy," Jeff taunted. "You're not going to lie around and watch TV all night, are you?"

"Maybe I am."

Jeff snuck up behind him, snatched the remote control and quickly flicked off the TV. He stood smack in front of Steven.

"Come on, get off your fat butt and play with me," Jeff pestered.

"Get out of my way," Steven ordered. He wanted to push Jeff away but he knew that if he did Jeff would push him back twice as hard. He hated being two years younger than his brother. He hated the fact that Jeff was stronger and much more aggressive.

"Come on," coaxed Jeff, leaping on Steven. He pinned his arms above his head and, straddling his knees on either side of Steven's chest, he bounced up and down, pressing his rear end into Steven's stomach.

Anger exploded inside Steven. "Get off!" With one swift move he brought his knee up as hard as he could and whacked Jeff in the small of his back. Jeff cried out in pain and fell onto the floor.

The boys heard their mum's heavy steps before her voice. "What's going on here?" she demanded.

Steven leapt off the couch and headed towards the back door. "I thought you wanted to play hockey?"

Jeff shot daggers at his brother and followed him out the door.

* * *

At dinner, Steven's mum brought the plates to the table. Steven sat slouched in his chair and slowly began poking at his food.

"Come on, Steven, you like chicken," Mrs. Edwards coaxed. "It is not a new recipe and it is not vegetarian."

Steven looked at his mum, suddenly hating the fact that she was so fit and conscientious. She taught Home Economics at the high school and was very big on healthy eating. Usually Steven loved to eat, but right now he just wanted to fade out.

Jeff jumped on the opportunity to tease his brother. "Maybe it's a good thing Mr. Lard-O doesn't want dinner. He might skate a little faster if he lost a few pounds."

Steven snarled back sarcastically, "Thank you, Mr. Perfect. You're a blue-eyed wonder and I wish I could be just like you."

"That's enough," Mrs. Edwards interrupted. Turning to Steven she continued, "You don't need to lose weight. You have a strong, sturdy build just like your dad. You may have my brown hair and eyes but you've got his strength." Turning to Jeff she laughed, "So, watch out big brother."

Steven had wanted to fade out of sight, but now his father sat smiling at him. "So," his Dad asked. "Do you think you made the team?"

Steven froze. He couldn't look at his father. He couldn't tell him.

"Yeah, I think so," Steven lied.

"When are they going to post the list?"

"Tomorrow," Steven lied again.

* * *

Later, when their parents had left the room and Steven was still poking at his food, he could feel his brother staring at him. "What?" he asked, annoyed.

"Do you really think you made it?"

Steven couldn't take it any more. "Shut up about the team," he snapped. "I didn't make it, okay? You're right. I'm just a big, fat, lazy wuss and I didn't make the rep team. Are you happy now? And if you tell Dad I'll kill you." Anger and disappointment welled up inside him. He swallowed hard, trying not to cry.

"Look. I'm sorry about the team, but you shouldn't have lied. Dad's going to find out anyway." When Steven didn't say anything, Jeff continued, "It won't be so bad. Who's your coach?"

Steven screwed up his face. "Carter, and his two bratty kids are on the *B* team, too."

"Hey, Carter's not so bad. He's tough, but that's what you need, and Josh is small but fast. He's a good player."

Steven put his elbows onto the table and let his head drop into his hands. He remembered the smirk on Josh's face when Steven missed his shot. "They say he's a bully and his brother is always sick," he complained. "Besides, now I won't get to go to Colorado."

Jeff tried to be optimistic. "You know, sometimes they pull guys up from the *B* team if someone drops out or gets injured. February is six months away."

"Fat chance," Steven replied. "There's just too many guys better than me."

"Maybe Dad will let you come to Colorado with us anyway. Ask him tomorrow." Jeff leaned into the table with a grin. "Come on, what do ya say?"

"What's the point if I can't play hockey?"

Jeff gave up. "Well then, play hockey and get better. Get tough."

"Bug off," Steven yelled after him as he left the room.

Sitting by himself at the table all Steven could think of was his dad and Jeff going off to Colorado. It was always Dad and Jeff, he told himself.

2

A Bad Start

N o!" Steven cried out when he heard his name. "Please, Mr. Sedgewick, can't I stay here? Isn't there anyone else you could move? *Pleeease* let me stay."

This was Steven's first year in grade seven at Hudson Middle School, and he'd been thrilled to be assigned to Mr. Barker's class. It was a great class with lots of athletic kids in it. The principal, Mr. Sedgewick, had warned them that he might have to shuffle a few people around, but Steven hadn't thought for one moment that it might be him. First of all he didn't make the peewee rep team, he thought angrily, and now he was being transferred to another home room! This was one list he didn't want to be on.

"Sorry, Steven, I know it's difficult, but I'm sure once you're settled you'll be happy in your new class." The principal's words were final. Steven knew there was no room for argument but he couldn't stop himself.

"My mum said that if I was moved from Mr. Barker's class she would phone the school board." He blurted out the lie without thinking.

Mr. Sedgewick looked down sternly at Steven. "Oh, did she really? Would you like me to give her a call?"

Steven didn't answer. When he had finally built up the courage to tell his dad about the team, Mr. Edwards had tried to hide his disappointment. He didn't ask when the list was posted, but Steven suspected he knew his son had lied. No, Steven didn't want Mr. Sedgewick to give his mum a call.

"Now, on your way," the principal ordered, interrupting Steven's thoughts.

Inside, Steven was screaming mad. Why me? Why was I the one who had to go? he wondered. It wasn't that Miss Drummond was so bad. He just didn't want to change classes.

Steven gathered up his books while glancing over at Will, who had a stupid look on his face as he wiggled his fingers to say goodbye. Will didn't look happy that Steven was going, but he was clearly delighted that he himself was staying.

Claire Andrews was sitting beside Will. She also gave Steven a wave and then her hand went back to twisting her hair which already sprung out in soft brown curls. Her cheeks were rosy as if she had just come off the ice. Steven wondered if it was his imagination or did she look sorry to see him go? As he left the room he could feel Claire's eyes on him and her image lingered in his mind.

* * *

It was the first practice, and Steven leapt onto the ice from the bench just as the Zamboni disappeared through the back of the rink. He loved to hear his blades scrape through the newly cleaned ice and feel the chilly air whip at his cheeks. He followed Will to the blueline, behind the goal post, and then circled back. They stopped at the face-off circle and dropped down to the ice to stretch their legs.

"Saint Louis drill," Coach Carter bellowed from the bench as he threw the pucks onto the ice. His hair was a cold grey, combed straight back off his face, and his eyes were anything but friendly. He had a broad, barrel-shaped chest and Steven knew he was one not to be messed with.

Each player skated up to the blueline and around the red dot, ready to receive the puck smacked out by the first skater from the right line. The sticks whacked the ice, the pucks rocketed through the air, and the players had to move fast to get into position.

Steven was just starting to loosen up as he raced to the blueline to receive a pass from Josh. Josh held back and the puck flew behind Steven. By the time he had retrieved the puck, Josh was approaching the blueline himself, ready to receive.

"Hurry up, man," he sneered at Steven.

Steven let it fly but missed the net by a long shot. Josh followed right behind and snapped the puck into the net, just missing Steven.

Nice guy, Steven thought sarcastically.

Coach Carter pushed them hard as he led them through several more drills. Steven could feel his muscles burning as he struggled to keep up.

"Edwards, get moving," the coach roared. "You're skating like a slug."

Steven knew it wasn't his imagination that every time Carter yelled at him, Josh smiled with pleasure. Steven's initial feeling of dislike for his teammate was turning into hatred.

In the locker room following the practice, Steven and Will sat next to each other on the bench listening to Mr. Carter.

"Okay, what I saw out there was a pretty poor performance," the coach roared. "Let's get a few things straight right from the start. First of all, you are to be here thirty minutes before practice, in the dressing room, and not one minute late. If you *are* late you'll do pushups. It's your responsibility and no one else's. Going to a Canucks game is not an excuse to miss my practice."

Geez, thought Steven. Every once in a while his dad got tickets to a Canucks game and he loved to watch the pros. He'd die if he got tickets for the Flyers and he couldn't go to watch Paul Coffey.

The coach continued, "The only excuse will be if you are sick or if you have a school commitment." He lifted his foot up onto a bench and leaned in over his thick thighs. Getting closer, he emphasized his words.

"It's a given that you have all your equipment here in good condition. That includes two sticks and sharp skates."

Steven and Will glanced at Amar at the same time. Will rolled his eyes and they both chuckled. They really liked Amar because he worked so hard at his hockey. He hadn't been playing long and up until now his equipment had all been second hand. This year it was all brand new, and top of the line. That, along with his handsome looks, made him appear ready for a TV advertisement.

"He looks good, but can he skate?" Will snickered in a whisper. Steven laughed out loud and Coach Carter glared at him.

"Eat at least two hours before a game, and it should be some type of carbohydrates, like pasta. Don't overeat or you'll skate like a barge. Lastly, but most importantly, you are to do exactly as I say, when I say. When I say stop — you stop. When I say go — you go. And when I say listen — you listen. You're here to play hockey, but I'll teach you my way. If you don't like it, you may as well walk right now. Got that, Edwards?"

All the players turned to look at Steven. Mortified, he wanted to disappear on the spot. Even after the coach had moved on, Steven still felt the humiliation burning on his face. Now the whole team will think I skate like a barge and don't pay attention, Steven thought in dismay.

* * *

Three weeks later, Steven was puffing as he and Will reached his house, which was at the top of the hill. The municipality of West Vancouver extended across the ridge of Hollyburn Mountain as it sloped down to the sea. It was a hard climb from the school but Steven loved to look back out across Burrard Inlet to the city itself. He saw several large freighters sitting still, high in the water, waiting to collect their cargoes of wheat or lumber. Numerous small sailboats were tacking their way around them, leaning in to catch the chilly wind. They contributed to Vancouver's picture postcard look. To-night was the first game of the season and even though they had been practising hard, Steven felt jittery.

"Do you want to shoot some pucks?" he asked.

"No, I gotta rest up," Will said seriously. "I want to get the first goal." He continued walking away from Steven, toward his house around the corner. Walking backward for a moment he called out, "Hey, let's make sure we're early. I want to be first on the ice."

Inside, Steven tried to do his homework but he couldn't concentrate. When Jeff came home he was happy to go out to the backyard and shoot with him.

"Look, you've got to be more aggressive if you want to score," Jeff whapped his stick at a tennis ball and sent it flying into the goal, scattering bright fallen leaves.

Steven frowned. "I'm on defence, not offence. I'm not *supposed* to score goals," he said, sticking up for himself.

"Everybody wants to score, that's what it's all about." Jeff tried to do some quick and fancy moves but Steven snatched the ball and scored.

"Nice shot. So who else is on defence besides you and Amar?"

"Sam Bacon, who's great. We call him Sizzler," Steven said with a smile. "He's got a great slap shot and he's a pretty high scorer for someone on defence."

"A defenceman who scores?" Jeff asked sarcastically.

"Yeah, yeah."

"Why don't you tell Carter you want to play offence. You've got to get tough."

"Oh right, as if I'm going to tell him anything. He says I'm big and defence is where I belong."

"Well, suit yourself."

"Besides, if I do get called to play rep, it will be on defence. They've already got a strong offence." The desire to play on the rep team and go to Colorado still nagged at Steven.

For a while, all that could be heard was the shuffling of feet and the sound of sticks whacking at the cement.

"So, how are you and Josh getting along?" Jeff asked, catching his breath.

Steven rushed at Jeff, trying to steal the ball, but his brother was too fast. "Josh is a bit like you," Steven said, annoyed that he didn't get the ball. "He's irritating and too pushy for me." Steven didn't give up.

"Sounds like my kinda guy, tough and ruddy," Jeff said, moving toward the net. This time Steven was there, blocking his shot.

"Did you know Josh and Andrew are twins?" Steven asked, beginning to puff.

"No way. Andrew looks more like you … like he's never going to make it to the end of the game."

"Ha! Ha! No really, he has asthma and when he skates too much he starts coughing and we all think he's going to drop dead. Andrew is our goalie, and he's the only one that Carter doesn't yell at. But he sure picks on Josh. And they both pick on me."

"As I said before, you've got to get tough. Carter just wants to see you working hard," Jeff warned, lifting his stick and blasting the ball into the net.

* * *

Will threw his gear into the car.

"You're dressed?" Steven observed in amazement.

Will answered seriously, "I want to be ready."

"We've still got lots of time," Steven said smiling, "Jeff says it's not cool to dress at home. He says it's better to dress with the team."

"I don't want to be cool." Will looked disgusted. "I want to play hockey."

* * *

Will was the first on the ice after the Zamboni and Steven was the last. He had been joking around with Shogo, who always made him laugh. Steven felt good just being around him. Suddenly he realized they were all ready and he wasn't.

"Edwards, this isn't a social gathering," Coach Carter roared. "Start thinking about the game."

It was only an exhibition game but it was against North Vancouver, the toughest team to beat in the city. This was the team that Steven and his teammates on West Van wanted to defeat most of all.

The puck dropped and Eric, West Van's centre, snared it and whipped it out to Will. Will did some fancy stick handling and carried the puck to the blueline. He passed it over to Josh and then followed it in front of the net. Josh advanced and then made a sweet pass back to Will, who saw an opening in North Van's defence and slapped the puck high into the corner of the net, scoring in the first minute of play.

"Wahoo!" Will raised his stick and shook it in victory. The team swarmed around, bumping him in jubilation. Will had wanted to score and he had, the first goal of the season.

North Van was not as pleased, however, and in their fury at letting in such a quick goal they seemed to grow in size. The mood was set. It was going to be a tough game. The puck dropped and once again Eric gave a swift pass to Will. North Van intercepted. Steven knew he had to get back down the ice.

"Edwards, skate," he heard Carter roar from the sidelines. Steven pushed hard, but his long strides made him look slow. Sizzler, skating backwards, stole the puck from the North Van forward and smacked it over to Steven. Steven took it behind the net and then looked for a pass. Josh was straight ahead on the inside of the blueline.

"Pass it," he screamed to Steven.

Steven pushed it off the boards but Josh missed it and North Van got possession. "Nice pass," Josh sneered.

With ten minutes to go in the second period, North Van scored a goal. The puck soared right over Andrew's shoulder and into the net. Two minutes later, they scored again.

Suddenly, Andrew was down on the ice. There was no one around him, Steven realized, so he couldn't have been hit. Something was wrong. He was tearing at his helmet and clutching his throat at the same time.

"Dad!" Josh screamed. Moving quickly, he pushed his way into the goal crease. He was trying to get his brother's helmet off when Coach Carter came in and helped him up.

Andrew was coughing and gasping at the same time. Carter handed him a puffer and encouraged him to take a few strong puffs. Andrew settled right down and stood quietly with his dad. The rest of the team stood back waiting, feeling badly for Andrew, knowing that Shogo could come on for him. Soon, however, father and son were nodding, and the coach turned away. Walking carefully on the ice, the coach returned to the bench, leaving Andrew to stay in the net.

For a moment no one spoke, no one moved. They couldn't believe he'd left Andrew in.

"Let's play hockey," Carter commanded. The game continued, and by the end of the second period the score was four to one for North Van.

Coach Carter was hopping mad and Steven felt like he was yelling at him the whole time. He could hear his voice bellowing even over the roar of the crowd. Everyone else could hear it too. "Edwards, *move* it! Get back down the ice!"

Out on the ice Josh echoed his dad's comments and Steven's anger was growing. Why didn't he just keep his trap shut? he wondered.

North Van scored twice in the third period and the game ended six to one. A cloud of disappointment hung over the dressing room as the players slowly undressed.

"Defence wins games," Carter boomed out in his husky voice. "You've got to be fast and you've got to be there."

He was talking to the whole team but Steven felt he was talking to him and the blood rose to his face. He caught a look from Josh and he wanted to smack him. Then Steven noticed Andrew. He looked small and pale and as though he was going to cry. Steven wondered if Andrew wanted to play hockey at all or if it was all Carter's idea. He couldn't help but feel that if Shogo had been in goal the score would have been different.

3

KABOOM

It was Saturday evening. Will and Steven were sprawled on the old brown sofa in Steven's family room watching a hockey game. Colorado and the Philadelphia Flyers were between periods, playing in Denver. Beads of sweat rippled across Paul Coffey's forehead and dripped down the side of his face. He was talking, clearly out of breath, and Steven hung onto his every word.

The camera followed Coffey back to the dressing room. As Steven watched he could hear in his mind the swish of the large hockey pants. He could hear the blades thudding over the wooden floors almost as though he, Steven Edwards, was walking through that door to the change room. He could even smell the gear soaked in sweat. It was so familiar. It was so great, he thought.

Steven's desire to go to Colorado in February still ached in his gut. Philadelphia was playing Colorado on the same weekend. He could be there. Right there in Denver, at the Coliseum, watching his team, the Flyers, and his man, Paul Coffey. Instead, it would be Jeff watching the Flyers and Jeff playing in the tournament in Colorado Springs. There was no way Steven was going to be moved up to the rep team. He wasn't playing well and he was sure his coach hated him. A low moan escaped him.

"What's your problem?" Will asked.

"You're lucky," Steven began slowly. "You're playing really well. You're the high scorer on the team and Carter loves you."

"Yeah, right," Will said with disbelief. His smile, however, reached right up into his eyes.

"You were awesome last game," Steven continued. "You're so good at manoeuvring your feet that you're hard to catch. It must be from all those years playing soccer."

Will lunged at Steven and punched him in the arm. Steven punched back and they rolled onto the floor.

"Hey, what are you punching me for? I said you were cool," Steven said, laughing, and scrambled back up on the couch. "It's too bad Josh can't get the puck into the net. If he could only let it rip like you."

Will looked pleased. "Yeah, if Josh could get more shots on goal we'd be laughing. He's in a real slump for someone who's supposed to be so good."

"Maybe if he'd stop mouthing off all the time, especially at me, he'd score more."

"You're right, he's a real dork. Even I find it annoying."

The phone interrupted their conversation. At the same time, Jeff came crashing into the room with his huge hockey bag slung over his shoulders. Brushing the walls, he manoeuvred his way into the kitchen. He dropped the bag with a thud and reached for the phone.

"Hello." A look of mischief came over Jeff's face as he listened. He sang into the phone, an octave too high, "Yes this is Steven. Is that you, Claire?"

In one swift move Steven leapt over the back of the couch and snatched the phone from his brother's hand.

Jeff let him take the receiver but, leaning over Steven's shoulder, he sang out, "I'd take you to the movies but you're tooooo ugly."

Steven elbowed Jeff with his free arm. His face turned bright red.

"Hello? Oh, hi Jen," he said, relieved it wasn't Claire. "I'm sorry. That was my jerk-face brother."

Jeff, puffed up as though he'd just been given a compliment, moved into the family room to watch the game.

Steven listened as Jen, Claire's best friend, asked what he and Will were doing on Hallowe'en. She asked if they could all go out in a group.

"Sounds cool," Steven answered, trying to sound calm while feeling a flutter ripple through him. "I'll ask Sizzler to come too."

Jen said she would ask a few more girls. Just before she hung up, she asked, "Oh, by the way, Steven, is there anyone that you like?"

Steven was glad she couldn't see his face turn red for the second time. "Who wants to know?"

Jen hesitated, "We all do."

Steven knew that Claire was right there. She probably had her ear to the phone, he guessed. There was no way he could say it. "I like a lot of people."

Jen sounded disappointed. "Well, how about Will? Who does he like?"

"You'll have to ask him." Before she could continue, Steven called out. "Hey, Will, Jen wants to ask you something."

There was a click and the phone went dead.

Suddenly there was a roar from the TV and all three boys focused back on the game. Coffey had scored! The Flyers were up by two.

"Yes!" the boys all cried out in unison. Jeff and Will slapped their hands together in victory.

The boys concentrated on the game for awhile until Jeff announced smugly, "Did you guys know you still have to go to your hockey practice on Hallowe'en?"

Steven was horrified. "No way! Carter wouldn't do that."

"Wrong-oh, bird brain. We found out at practice tonight. All practices are on."

"I'm not going," Steven said, crossing his arms in defiance. "Carter can stuff it. We only have Hallowe'en once a year. I'll just tell him I'm sick."

"Yeah, right. Sick on Hallowe'en. Real smart, Einstein. As if he'd believe you," his brother warned.

"Well then, we should all boycott it. None of us should go," Stephen replied.

"Hey, man, don't have a super spaz," Jeff said, trying to calm Steven down. "Look, practice is from four-thirty to six-thirty. You could be on the road by seven."

"But we have to be home by nine for Dad's fireworks. He's the one who will have a super spaz if we're late."

As the next two weeks rolled by, Steven got more and more excited each day. He thought about the stash of firecrackers he had in his room. He knew he wasn't supposed to have them and that his mum would freak out if she knew, but it was going to be awesome. Besides, they were only crackling apples and a few bombs. Every year his dad put on a huge display of fireworks and this year Steven would have his own supply to surprise him with. Fireworks were a Vancouver tradition and it was the part about Hallowe'en that Steven loved the best. He couldn't wait.

* * *

Finally, Hallowe'en arrived. The sharp autumn air pinched Steven's cheeks as he walked home from school. Drifting clouds hung low in the sky and it already seemed dark and eerie. It was a perfect night for Hallowe'en. If only they didn't have to go to hockey. The urge for Steven to phone and tell Coach Carter that he was sick was strong, but Jeff was right. That would be a lie he couldn't get away with. Maybe, he hoped, the coach would let them go early.

Carter worked them hard in the practice and Steven's insides were racing as he sped through the drills. He felt aggressive and pushed himself, willing the practice to be over so that they could be gone. His body reacted in tune with his mood and he played well, liking the way it felt.

The only member missing was Andrew. It must be awful to be sick a lot, Steven sympathized, especially when you had to miss great times like Hallowe'en.

In the dressing room the atmosphere buzzed with excitement as everyone hurried to get out as soon as possible. Steven was the first one dressed and ready. He was waiting for Will and Sizzler when Josh approached him.

"Hey, man, what's up?" Josh asked, full of himself.

"What do you mean?" Steven stiffened, afraid of what was to come.

"Are you guys going out?"

"No," Steven lied, but Josh pressed on.

"I've got some great stuff that I bought in the States." He raised his eyebrows and bobbed his head. "Bottle rockets, mighty mites, and crackling bombs."

The last thing Steven wanted to do was go out with Josh. He could take his stupid rockets and send himself to the moon, he thought to himself.

Sizzler joined them and, as he dropped down his bag, Josh turned to him. "Sizzler, mind if I come along tonight? Andrew's sick, so we can't go out."

"It's okay by me," Sizzler answered in his normally good-natured way.

Steven knew he was beaten.

* * *

Within half an hour everyone met at Steven's house. The girls were all dressed as witches. Will was wearing his pads and a hockey jersey. Sizzler was a bum dressed in rags. He had sprayed his hair grey and it stuck out in matted tufts. Josh was wearing a referee shirt and had a whistle in his mouth and Steven was a thug dressed in black.

As soon as his house was out of sight, Steven reached into his pack and pulled out some of his crackling apples. He lit the wick and threw them into the street. There was a huge bang followed by a series of loud popping noises that sounded like gunfire. Steven beamed. This was too much fun!

"Is that the best you can do?" Josh asked, bumping into Steven as they ran up to the next house. He held out his bag and asked for extra treats for his sick brother.

Steven was fuming. Why did Josh have to come anyway, he thought. He's going to wreck everything. Steven didn't believe for a minute that Andrew would see one bit of candy. As the group crowded around the door, each waiting for their loot, Josh closed his bag and ran ahead.

Turning the corner onto a new street, Steven noticed Josh standing at the bottom of the nearest driveway. He was waving at them frantically, indicating that they should hurry. The girls began walking up the driveway.

"No, no!" Josh whispered loudly. "I don't think we should do this house. Come on," he ordered, still waving for them to hurry. "Quick, hide behind this bush."

Everyone followed Josh's example and crouched down behind him. They watched the front door of the house they had just missed when suddenly — KABOOM! The pumpkin that had been burning on the front step blew up and the pieces flew in all directions. Everyone bolted toward the next block, running as fast as they could.

The whole gang was out of breath, gasping for air and howling. Caught up in the excitement, Steven's heart was racing. That was awesome, he had to admit. They carried on and went to a few more houses, but collecting candy suddenly seemed dull. Steven wasn't going to let Josh outdo him, especially in front of Claire.

Steven spotted his target — a series of three pumpkins sitting on a front porch. Josh spotted them at the same time.

Steven spoke like a villain about to attack his next victim. "These are mine," he bragged.

"Yeah, what are you going to blow them up with? Those wussy crackling things?" Josh asked, and everybody laughed.

They crossed the street and Steven took off his pack, placed it on the ground, and pulled out three bombs. He knew he should save them to show his dad, especially since he hadn't tried them out. What if they were dangerous? What if they didn't work? he worried. Then he would really look like a fool.

"Eww, those look scarey," Josh teased, looking into the pack to see if there were any more. "Do you think baby powder will make a bang?" Josh took his remaining bottle rockets and put them into Steven's pack. "My bag's busting. Do you mind?"

Yes, I do mind, Steven thought, but he was already heading back toward the porch. He crouched down below the windows and snuck up to the pumpkins. Steven took the lids off carefully and blew out each candle. He was scared, but he couldn't stop now. He felt all the eyes watching him from across the street: Josh's eyes, Claire's eyes — especially Claire's.

He had to do it. Steven placed a bomb in each pumpkin and pulled out his matches. His hand was shaking. He lit the first wick. Now he had to work fast to light the others and run before the first one exploded. He lit the second wick. As his hand went into the third pumpkin his saw the headlights coming towards him. His hand hit the side of the pumpkin and the match went out.

"Runnnn!" came a wild cry from across the road.

As Steven flew off the porch he heard the explosion.

KABOOM! KABOOM!

He tore off after the others through a hedge, across the alley, through two more backyards and down to the creek.

Out of the corner of his eye he had seen pieces of the pumpkins fly. Two policemen had jumped out of their car but Steven was sure they hadn't see him.

Claire looked at Steven with admiration as they hurried along the street back to his house. "Fireworks scare me, but that was awesome. Weren't you frightened?"

"No," he said, knowing he was now safe.

Mr. Edwards had bought oodles of fireworks and Steven felt proud as they all gathered around watching the sparks explode into the darkness in a spray of colours. He worried about his firecrackers and hoped his pack would still be where he'd left it at the side of the road.

After the fireworks, they moved inside for hot chocolate. Claire and Jen flopped down on one of the comfy couches that lined the basement family room. Steven and Will sat down beside them, one on either end. Loud music filled the air. As Steven pretended to lean across the girls and talk to Will, he slipped his arm up around the back of the couch and behind Claire. Steven suddenly had this great desire to kiss her but he was paralyzed by the thought of it. At the sound of his dad coming down the stairs, he whipped his arm away. Will followed his lead and dropped Jen's hand. His face turned bright red.

"Steven!"

The anger in his father's voice, the look on his face, and the backpack clutched in his hand, filled Steven with terror.

"There is a policeman at the door who would like to speak with you."

4

A Colourful Game

Steven stared at the brass buttons on the officer's coat. Of course, he had to admit it was his pack. His name and address were in it — that's how the policeman had found him.

Steven's bottom lip quivered, but the lie came easily.

"Yes, it is my backpack, but the firecrackers belong to someone else. I took them because his bag broke."

The officer did not look convinced. "Who do the firecrackers belong to?"

"I can't tell you that, sir."

Mr. Edwards interrupted, "Tell the officer what he needs to know, Steven."

Steven stood silently. It hurt to breathe. He hated Josh, but he wasn't going to rat on him. Besides, then he'd have to admit to his own prank. He couldn't do that in front of his dad.

The officer continued, "Do you know that the use of firecrackers is against the law unless supervised by an adult?"

"Yes, sir." Steven said quietly, the words heavy in his throat.

"Did you blow up any pumpkins tonight?"

"No, sir."

"Did you see your friend blow up any pumpkins?"

"No, sir."

"I can't say that I believe you." The officer stared at Steven, letting him squirm in the silence. Finally he continued, "… but I have no proof. Your name will be placed on file and I suggest you stay away from firecrackers in the future."

Steven's eyes dropped to the floor. A new panic swept over him, knowing he had to face his dad. He didn't move, even after the door had closed.

His father's voice was slow and deliberate. "I think it's time your friends went home."

Steven slowly lifted his head to look at his father. He wished he hadn't. His expression was hardened with disappointment.

"When they have gone, go to your room. I'll get Jeff to help me clean up."

* * *

Steven sat on his bed as the same thoughts tumbled over and over again in his head. Why had he been so stupid? he wondered. This was all Josh's fault. If it wasn't for him, none of this would have happened. With each thought the anxiety grew. His dad would come soon. Steven was dreading that moment when his bedroom door opened.

Mr. Edwards started calmly, in a deliberately low voice. "Who were you with? Where did you go? Where did you get the stuff?" he demanded. As he continued asking questions his voice got louder and his eyes grew wider.

Steven was frantic. He didn't want to say the wrong thing.

Finally, Mr. Edwards exploded. "These aren't difficult questions, Steven."

His dad knew what had happened, he had figured it out. All he wanted was the truth, Steven guessed, but he just couldn't give it.

* * *

It was 5:30 a.m. when Steven crawled out of bed for his early morning practice. As he opened the front door, the icy November air bit at his face and woke him right up. He glanced up at the North Shore mountains that formed a backdrop to the city of Vancouver. Vancouver had a mild climate, but from November to March the mountains were often covered in snow. The ski hills were only minutes away and it was like being able to ski in your own backyard. That morning the hills were bare. It had been a week since Hallowe'en and Steven could still see the look on his dad's face. He knew his chances of going to Colorado were getting slimmer and slimmer. If only there was something that he could do right, he thought.

Maybe he should ask Claire to the movies, Steven told himself. He had missed her being on the team but had understood when she said she had wanted to play some sports for the school. Hockey was a full time commitment. Ever since Hallowe'en, he and Claire had been a kind of an item. The girls all said that they were 'going together.' It felt good.

* * *

Steven pushed the door into the dressing room and was immediately hit with the smell of old sweat. The guys were laughing and someone was ripping velcro straps. He loved being there and forgot about everything else.

Will, who the boys had voted team captain, was trying to get the West Vancouver players focused. "Hey, guys, we're playing North Van again on Saturday night and we can win."

"Yeah," they all nodded in agreement.

Josh had been doing up his skates with a fierce intensity, not saying much. He had only scored one goal this season and wanted more. Will often passed it to him but Josh couldn't seem to get it in. Josh suddenly snarled at Steven, "If you'd get back down the ice a little faster maybe we could stop these guys."

Under his breath, intending only Will to hear, Steven taunted, "Why don't you sit on one of your mighty mites?"

"KABOOM," Shogo said, projecting his voice and making everyone laugh.

Just as they were leaving, Sizzler came charging into the dressing room with his hair sticking out in all directions. Coach Carter, who had come in to help Andrew with his goalie gear, looked at his watch with a stern expression. "Better get a new alarm clock, Bacon. Yours seems to be a little slow."

"Sorry, Coach. I'm all dressed — I just got to put on my skates." Huffing from hurrying, he dove into his bag.

"It'll cost you twenty pushups before you start the drill. Move it!" the coach barked.

* * *

Saturday night arrived and West Van was desperate for a win. The team had lost their first four games of the season, tied one and then won the next two. If they could only beat North Van, they would have a chance to get into the playoffs. As Steven and Will approached the dressing room they heard the guys laughing behind the door. Inside, Sizzler was the centre of attention. He had dyed his hair a bright orange and it stuck out in wild tufts.

"It's going to bring us good luck, you'll see: North Van's going down. Yeah!" Sizzler hollered.

Shogo, holding an empty cola can in his hand, was letting out a loud series of belches and enjoying each one. Steven opened his bag and, as he began to dress, he could feel the tension building. They were going to beat these guys! he told himself.

With ten minutes to go, Coach Carter came in for the team talk. "I want to see some smart hockey out there. Stick with your checks and stay on top of them. Hold your positions and remember what we did in practice. I want to see some good fast skating." His strong voice bellowed out in all directions. "Will, Josh and Eric: You'll play first line. Bacon and Edwards: You're on defence. Shogo's in goal and I want to see some defence in there helping him out."

"Coach," Steven interrupted. "Could I play offence?"

Carter ignored the question for the time being, but his eyes focused on Steven.

"You guys can beat this team. But you've got to be better on the power play, better on *defence* — just plain better. They're a tough team but you can do it. Now get out there and show me that you know how to play hockey."

Steven felt it was up to him, and him alone, to defend their goal. His stomach churned.

It was obvious that West Van was on a mission right from the opening whistle. They seemed to be everywhere at once, but the swift-skating North Van team was right on them. North Van's number four, the fastest skater on their team, belted down the ice, with Josh right on his tail. Just as he went for the shot, Josh crosschecked him and sent him crashing into the boards. The puck hit the post and Josh got two minutes in the box.

The battle carried on. Every time West Van would get down into their end North Van would take it back. But each time Steven was there. Up and down, back and forth. West Van had ten shots on goal but no score.

Steven's thighs were burning and sweat was trickling into his eyes. It was the last period, two minutes to go. There was a scramble in the corner boards. Josh was beating off both defencemen, slapping for the puck. Will was in front of the net. Josh took an elbow in the head and crashed to the ice. As he went down, his stick flicked the puck out to Will who smoked it in past a bewildered goalie. West Van won, one to zero.

The game was a shutout for Shogo, but Steven felt great too. He knew he had defended the goalie well. Carter didn't say much but he didn't yell at him either. Things were looking up.

Back in the dressing room the boys went wild, punching the air in rapid succession.

"Yes, yes, yes!" Sizzler cried out. "That was awesome. I know what it was. It was my hair. I'm going to keep it like this for the rest of the season." He slid his hand down the back of his head. His hair was stuck to his head with sweat.

"I don't know, Bacon," Shogo shouted. "I think that next game it should be a different colour. Maybe blue or purple. What do you think, boys?"

"Yeah, we'll call him rainbow man," Will called out, laughing. "I think rainbow man needs a shampoo, boys, don't you?"

Steven watched as Shogo wrapped his arm around Sizzler's neck, holding it in a vise-like grip, and started dragging him off towards the shower. Will and Josh rushed in to help. Amar came up with some shampoo and followed Sizzler as he screamed and kicked and tried to get free.

Once in the shower stall, Will gave the orders. "Drop him and hold him."

Amar rubbed some shampoo into Sizzler's hair and watched his own hands turn orange.

"Okay, on three. Steven are you ready?"

"Ready, set," he answered.

"One, two, *three*," Will commanded, and the water streamed down on Sizzler.

Steven was pumped as he and Will left the rink. What a game! he thought with a grin. He laughed out loud remembering Sizzler with orange dye dripping down his face.

There was another reason why Steven was excited. He had just heard a rumour. A defenceman on the rep team was moving to Edmonton after Christmas and they would be looking for a replacement. If Steven continued to play like he did tonight, he dreamed, he might just have a chance.

5

Bad Decisions

It was after the next practice when Coach Carter announced that he had arranged for the team to play an exhibition game the Saturday before Christmas. "I've talked to all your parents and it seems the only one who can't make it is Edwards," he concluded.

Steven couldn't believe it. That was the only weekend that his dad could take off work and go with them to Whistler, a fabulous mountain resort ninety minutes north of Vancouver. It was still raining in Vancouver but Whistler had mega centimetres of snow. It might be Steven's only chance to ski with his dad all year.

Carter continued, "We're moving into the end of the season and then the playoffs are in February. You guys are looking sharp but we need more practice."

Steven groaned. "Coach, couldn't you make it another day?"

Coach Carter's steel eyes latched onto Steven's like a vise. "No. It's all arranged. Is where you are going, Edwards, more important than hockey?"

"No, sir."

"Maybe you should think about it. You were just starting to pick up." He turned his back on Steven and strutted out of the dressing room.

Steven felt deflated. He couldn't let his dad down again. Besides, the game didn't count and he wanted to go skiing.

* * *

This Christmas, Steven had managed to get everyone a present and he had done it all himself. He had saved up his allowance and some extra money earned doing chores. The only person he had missed was Claire and now he was broke. He wished he hadn't used up all of his cash.

In the kitchen, waiting to go to Whistler, Steven saw the answer. It was a ten dollar bill all folded up in a little square just lying on the counter. He stopped, his feet suddenly stuck to the floor, and stared at the bill. His eyes quickly scanned the room and he held his breath as he listened carefully. No one was around. Before he could think it through clearly, his hand shot out. He grabbed the money and shoved it into his pocket.

The car honked and Jeff hollered, "Hurry up, Dad's waiting!"

At the same time, his mum came into the kitchen. "Steven, have you seen a ten dollar bill?" she asked. "It was folded. I was sure I left it here on the counter."

His dad honked again. "No, Mum," he said quickly. "Come on, we've got to go."

"Are you sure? I know it was here."

"I'll ask Jeff," Steven said, looking away from her eyes.

"Don't bother, I'll ask him."

* * *

The day was dull and grey and that's just how Steven felt as they sped along the winding road on their way to Whistler. Something was not right about this weekend, Steven worried.

Maybe he should have stayed home. He was going to be the only one to miss the game.

Steven had a great day on the mountain with his family, but during the afternoon hockey kept creeping into his thoughts. How had the team done without him? he wondered. How angry was Carter? Who had Josh picked on without Steven being there? He couldn't shake it.

After dinner he turned to his brother. "Hey, Jeff, do you want to go over to the lake and shoot some pucks? I hear it's frozen solid."

"Nah, I think I'll watch a movie."

"Please," begged Steven. "We brought our skates and I need to practice."

"Okay," Jeff gave in and the boys headed off to Lost Lake which was a ten minute walk from their cabin.

There was a layer of snow on top of the ice and the boys began scraping it off with their sticks, making an area on which to play. They pushed the snow up into a pile behind their makeshift goal to help stop the low pucks. Other boys joined them and soon they had enough guys to get a good game going.

Steven watched his brother leap into action as he fired shot after shot into the net. Their side was winning eight to two. Skates flashed and scraped over the bumpy ice and with each breath the cold winter air filled their lungs. Steven thought he was doing okay on defence, but he wanted to score. Jeff must have read his mind because he started to coach.

"Shoot the puck hard and low and make sure you get it around the guy who's checking you. Shoot to score!" Jeff encouraged. It was times like these that Steven almost liked having Jeff as a brother.

The next day was another great one and Steven felt better. Just before they were ready to head back to Vancouver he thought about the ten dollar bill that was still folded up inside his wallet.

"I need to go buy something before we leave," Steven told his parents and hurried off toward the nearby Whistler Village. It resembled a Swiss ski village with picturesque chalets hanging over streets lined with outdoor cafes and shops.

In one of the shops his eyes fell on a small white bear wearing a toque and skis. Perfect, he said to himself. He took out the folded bill and put it on the counter.

Suddenly, Jeff was right beside him, leaning over the counter. "So, who's the bear for?"

Steven ignored him.

"Let me guess. It's a girl. Her name starts with *C*? She has freckles on her nose and looks like a pixie."

"She does not look like a pixie. Bug off, will you?"

"Hey, nice trick with the money. How'd you get it all folded like that? It looks like you were practising your Japanese paper folding."

Steven unfolded the bill and handed it to the woman at the counter. He took the package and went out the door, but he felt no pleasure in buying the gift. Instead, he was filled with a depressing heaviness. He had an urge to take the bear back and retrieve the ten dollars but Jeff was right behind him. He felt sick about taking his mother's money. Steven wished he had stayed home and played hockey.

* * *

When they got back to West Vancouver Steven phoned Will right away.

"How was the game?"

"We lost." Will said with disappointment. "The coach said it was our defence. We needed you, pal."

Steven groaned into the phone.

"However, there is some good news," Will added, his voice perking up.

"Carter's booked us a tournament in Kelowna in a couple of weeks. We're going on a real road trip."

"All right!" Steven's spirits lifted. He loved the small interior town that was situated in the Okanagan valley right on Okanagan Lake.

"And."

"And what?"

"And, the rep team *is* scouting for a defenceman to take to Colorado."

6

Can't Win for Losing

Steven and Jeff followed closely behind their father on their
way to a Canucks game. The cars rushed by as the crowd
moved along the side of the bridge that led to Vancouver's
spectacular dome, GM Place. Steven felt his excitement
building as they approached the gate.

Once inside, the noise level rose. A young man wearing a
Canucks hat was yelling, "Programs, programs, get your programs." The air smelled of hot dogs and popcorn and suddenly Steven felt hungry.

Trying to avoid the crowd, Steven bumped into Jeff who
immediately bumped him back. Steven met his brother's eyes
and knew that he was about to be tackled. Their dad also saw
the look.

"Hey, guys, try not to embarrass me," he warned. They
moved along in the stream, sharing the excitement.

Jeff raised his eyes at Steven and, with a nod, directed him
to run ahead. "Let's find our seats," he whispered. "Dad will
find us."

Steven looked down at his ticket to check on their section
when Jeff suddenly lunged at him. He grabbed his shoulders
and pinned him behind a pillar.

"What the … ?" Steven began as he fell against the cold
cement.

Jeff still pinned him back with one hand as he peered around the pillar in the direction from which they had come.

"Carter! I'm sure I saw Carter. He just passed us. Man, I hope he didn't see you."

Steven felt the colour drain from his face "Are you sure? Did he see you?"

"No, I think he missed us. But geez, Steven, what were you thinking? I told you not to lie to Dad, not to tell him your practice was cancelled. You should have gone. What if Dad sees him?"

"I don't care," Steven shot back. "He shouldn't be here anyway. If *he* doesn't have to be at the practice, why should *I*?" As Steven spoke, his eyes scanned the crowd. There was no sign of Coach Carter but he saw his dad coming towards them.

"There you are." Mr. Edwards looked at Steven. "You look a little pale, son. Are you feeling okay?"

"Fine, I'm fine. Maybe I'm just a little hungry."

"Of course you are. You're always hungry!" he laughed.

As the players came onto the ice Steven could feel the goose bumps growing on his skin. The Canucks came out first, followed by the Flyers. It was so great to see these guys in real life — in flesh and blood, Steven thought. He could hear their voices, hear their movements — it was as though he could reach out and touch them. The only problem was that Steven loved both teams. Vancouver was his hometown, and he felt he had to be loyal. On the other hand, Paul Coffey was his all-time favourite player. How could he not want him to win? Steven wondered. He sat forward in his seat, trying to catch every move. He wished he could skate like that.

The puck dropped at centre ice and the game began. At the end of the first period, Steven sat back feeling spent. His throat was dry from screaming and he was dying for a drink. "Dad …" he started.

"Yeah yeah." His father smiled and reached into his pocket.

Steven was just about to take the money when Jeff reached over and snatched it. He pushed Steven back into his seat with his eyes bugged out, warning him to stay put. "I'll get the drinks."

"I've got to come out 'cause I have to go to the washroom," Steven insisted, bugging his eyes back at Jeff.

As soon as they were out in the foyer, Jeff turned to Steven. "Are you nuts? Don't you remember who's here?"

"Yeah, I know, but I have to pee. I'll be careful and meet you back at our seats."

Steven pulled his Flyers hat down over his face and slunk towards the men's room. Once inside he quickly scanned the room. Whew, no one was there that he recognized, so he did his thing and left.

Steven walked carefully back through the crowd. He was feeling tense and irritable and beginning to wish he had gone to the practice when someone suddenly grabbed his arm. "Hey, Edwards, what are you doing here?" The voice was deep and gruff but Steven knew instantly whose it was.

"Bug off," Steven yelled, pushing his brother's hand off his arm.

"Hey, you're spilling our drinks," Jeff cried. He followed Steven as he scuttled up the stairs and into the section. "Ha, ha, gotcha!"

The next two periods weren't as exciting as the first, and Steven found his eyes scanning the crowd in the huge stadium. The Canucks held a two-goal lead until near the end of the third period, when Pavel Bure blasted a shot right into the goal mouth to clinch the win. Steven was glad the game was over.

Once outside, Steven was happy to feel the cold January rain. He disappeared into his jacket and shuffled along to their car. The evening hadn't turned out the way he had thought it would.

* * *

The next night, Steven was sitting in the dressing room waiting for Will. He hadn't seen him all day and was anxious to hear about the practice he had missed the night before. He heard Coach Carter's voice outside the door and immediately dropped his head, pretending to tighten his skates. Carter pushed his way into the room and Steven could feel his powerful presence. He was afraid to look up. He held his breath, waiting for what was to come.

"Edwards, get your butt out there on the ice. I want to see some hard skating tonight." That was it. He was gone.

Why didn't he say anything about being at the hockey game? Steven worried. He's probably just waiting for me to get in front of everyone before he yells at me. The thought of being humiliated in front of his friends rippled through him, intensifying his fear. He wanted to bolt but he headed out onto the rink. Where was Will? Steven wondered. He needed Will to be there.

Down on the ice, Steven joined the others as they did their beginning stretches. Then he followed Sizzler around in the figure eight to continue stretching his arms and legs. He lifted his stick up above his head and then down behind his back. He dropped down, dragging one leg behind him, and then switched to the other leg. Steven liked doing these exercises. They were familiar and that gave him confidence. Suddenly, Will was beside him.

"Where were you?" Steven demanded.

Before Will had a chance to answer, Sizzler shouldered him as he skated past. "Hey, loser, try and get here on time,

Will ya?" He had a big grin on his face and they all laughed, knowing it was Sizzler who was usually late.

The team lined up in the corner behind the goal line, ready to start the cross-over drill. Steven was still thinking about Carter. He pushed hard as he moved backwards towards the blueline, his skates scraping into the ice. He slammed the ice with his stick and then slammed the stick against the boards. Crossing one skate over the other, he moved sideways across the blueline while still facing the goal until he slammed the boards with his stick on the other side. Backwards to the red line. Slam the boards. Cross-over sideways to the other side. Slam the boards. Steven loved the slam. He loved the noise and the vibration of his stick in his hand when he did it.

Back in line, Will whispered so the others couldn't hear. "You were lucky. Carter wasn't here last night."

"Yeah, right, real lucky," Steven answered sarcastically. "He was at the hockey game and I think he saw me."

Will looked at him as though he was crazy. "What are you talking about? He was at the hospital with Andrew."

"What?" Steven felt the relief flush through his body. It was replaced with anger. "I'm going to kill my brother," he said through clenched teeth. It took him a minute before he realized what Will had said.

"What's the matter with Andrew?"

"He couldn't breathe. You know, this asthma thing. Carter had to rush him into Emergency."

"Geez, the poor guy. Is he okay?" Steven felt guilty as his own fears decreased and he realized that it was a result of Andrew not being well. "I hope he's all right."

"Well, Carter's here, so he must be." They were both quiet for a few moments until Will spoke again. "It's too bad you missed the practice, though."

"Why?" Steven asked curiously.

"Well, since Carter wasn't here, Coach Linden from the rep team took the practice. He was scouting for his new defenceman. He should have seen you."

"No!" Steven let his disappointment escape loudly as he slapped his stick repeatedly against the ice. "Geez, I can't win for losing."

At that moment Josh joined the line. Hearing what Steven had said brought life to his pale green eyes. "That's because you are a *loser*," he said with a smirk.

Steven felt himself snap. He pulled back his stick and slashed out.

In an instant, Will slid in between them, knocking the stick down. "Cool it, Steven, he's not worth it."

Steven pushed Will back and thrust his face up to Josh. "I'll get you, Carter. One day I'll get you."

"Oooh, tough guy." Josh said, still smirking. "Mr. Cream Puff is turning into Mr. Tough Guy." He thrust his gloves forward and, hitting Steven's chest pad, he pushed himself backwards, turned and skated over to the bench where the coach was waving them in.

Steven's jaw was clenched and he could feel the blood throbbing against the inside of his helmet. "Geez, I hate that guy. I tell ya, Will, I'm gonna get him."

7

A Road Trip to Kelowna

The bell rang and Steven grabbed his books and headed for the hall. He automatically looked to the second locker from the end. Claire waved as he passed her. Steven could see the little bear propped up on the top shelf and he smiled back. "See ya," he said, feeling pumped.

It was the second week in January and the air was so cold that it stung the insides of his nostrils when he breathed. Steven hadn't bothered to put on his coat and he shivered as he climbed into the van where Will, his mother and Steven's mother were waiting. Their two huge hockey bags and the four weekend bags took up a lot of space in the back of the van, but Steven and Will made themselves comfortable with a tall stack of comics.

It took them two hours to pass through the farm country near Chilliwack and along the Fraser River to Hope. It was there that they began the steep climb up into the mountains along the Coquihalla Highway. Tiny flakes of snow, like bits of ash floating down from a chimney, fell gently onto the windshield, and the boys noticed that the snow at the side of the road got deeper and deeper as they climbed into the mountains. There was something magical about snow, Steven thought.

Finally they drove across the floating bridge that spanned Okanagan Lake and brought them into the picturesque city of Kelowna. Mrs. Edwards drove straight to the downtown hotel.

They climbed out of the van and the light dry snow squeaked beneath their feet. It was about twelve degrees below zero and the freezing air gripped their throats and pierced through their clothes into every inch of their bodies.

In the lobby a huge fireplace with bright orange flames blazed out a warm welcome. There were three large, over-stuffed sofas all facing each other and, in the middle, there was a large round table with a beautiful vase and arrangement of flowers. A few of the players were sunk into the sofas.

Shogo stood up as soon as he noticed Steven. "Coach Carter said we were to drive to Winfield as soon as everyone arrived. He, Josh and Andrew have already gone out to the rink."

"Who's missing?" Steven asked.

"Only Sizzler. We'll have to leave without him."

It was already after five o'clock and, since it was a twenty-minute drive to the arena, everyone left immediately. Mrs. Edwards drove cautiously as they made their way to the small community of Winfield, where the tournament was being held.

When they arrived, the first thing they saw was a huge banner stretched across the entrance to the arena: *WINFIELD WELCOMES WEST VANCOUVER, WILLIAMS LAKE, PENTICTON, ARMSTRONG and VERNON*. It didn't matter where they were, Steven thought, he liked the feeling of a new rink. Everything was the same and yet different. He walked down a long hallway with cement walls covered with pictures of winning teams. He passed a glassed-in display of trophies and medals. In the distance he could hear the hum of the Zamboni cleaning the ice and the smell of french fries hung in the air.

Steven loved the familiar smell of the dressing room. Even though it stunk, it got him pumped, got him thinking about the game. The bragging and belching began as Steven started to dress. It felt good to rip the tape and wrap it around his socks. The sounds, the smells — everything was so cool.

Excitement was building as they dressed. Ten minutes before they were to go out on the ice, Coach Carter came in to give the pep talk. Sizzler had arrived just in time. The room was suddenly quiet as the team waited to hear the lines. It had already been decided that Andrew would be in the pipes but Shogo was dressed and ready as a backup.

"I want to see some smart passing," the coach began. "Be thinking all the time. Watch where your teammates are and try to anticipate their moves." The team was sitting on the bench and Carter was moving slowly back and forth in front of them as he spoke in his rough voice, looking each player in the eye, making them feel like he was talking only to them.

"Know where to pass and be there to be passed to. For heaven's sake, don't hog the puck. Move it around." He stopped and all eyes were on him. Looking straight at Steven, he added, "Defence, play smart and be all over your man. We can't win without good defence." Suddenly his eyes softened and a smile spread over his face. "Now get out there and play hockey."

Winfield's centre looked tough. Number ten was broad and meanness oozed out from under his plastic face guard. The puck dropped. Eric, West Van's centre, snatched it and whipped it out to Will, who flew with it down to the blueline and made a slick pass to Josh. Will went around the net ready to receive. Josh charged the net but lost the puck to a defence-man who cleared it out on the right boards. Winfield's defence was fierce as they kept the puck out to the sides and then kept slamming West Van against the boards. Josh appeared to be loving it as he slammed right back. Suddenly, the referee's hand went up. A penalty against Winfield.

Back at centre, Eric grabbed the puck and made a quick pass to Josh. Josh passed to Will, whose stick-handling was awesome as he zigzagged around the defence and hammered the puck into the net for a power play goal.

West Van held the lead right into the third period. Steven was playing tough, getting the puck out and back down the ice. Winfield far outnumbered them in penalties but West Van had only managed the one power play goal, and they were starting to wear down under the bashing. With ten minutes left in the third period, Winfield charged the net but Andrew deflected the puck, making an awesome save. A face-off in the bottom left circle was called in West Van's end. Steven moved into the circle to cover Winfield's left wing.

Winfield's big centre bent over the puck for the face-off and sneered at Eric. "Too bad the pretty city boy doesn't know how to play hockey."

Eric didn't hesitate, "You're so ugly I'll bet they make you sleep in the barn." The big centre snatched the puck and scored for Winfield. The roar of the home crowd was wild as he barged past Steven and scored again.

That was it, Steven was mad. He called after the centre, "You're snorting so much your muzzle's fogging up." The banter wasn't helping the score, but it sure felt good.

Determined not to let anything else by, Steven and Sizzler attached themselves like glue. Nothing else got past them, but the whistle blew and Winfield won, two to one.

* * *

The hotel had provided a team room where the guys gathered around the TV and quietly ate their pizza. It had been a busy day and they were exhausted. Steven didn't mind when Coach

Carter told them they had to be in bed, with lights out, by ten. He knew the next morning's game started at seven o'clock and that meant he would have to be up by at least five.

The only one to complain was Sizzler. "Hey, I wanted to explore."

"It's okay," said Steven, letting out a big yawn, "We can explore tomorrow. The only thing I want to explore right now is my bed."

"But there's a heated outdoor pool and a hot tub, both with gobs of steam pouring out of them. There's a mini mall attached to the hotel and it has a joke shop and a bowling alley."

"Tomorrow, Sizzler, tomorrow," Will said, standing up. "We've got to play a game of hockey first. Then we can go bowling."

8

A Joke on Josh

The alarm woke him from his sleep. Steven bolted out of bed in a panic. For a second he felt lost in a space twice the size of his room at home. It was pitch black and all he could see was the green illuminated numbers of the alarm clock. Five thirty. A hotel room with his mum lying in the bed next to him. It all clicked into place. Kelowna, hockey, now! Steven remembered. He groped his way into the bathroom where his gear was hanging from every available spot in order to air out.

The team met down in the lobby for muffins and juice. Outside, the freshly fallen snow illuminated the darkness; Kelowna was still at rest. The sky had a hint of warm pink suggesting that the sun would soon be rising.

The banner still stretched across the entrance of the Winfield rink to welcome them and, even though they had only been there once, there was a feeling of familiarity. They were playing Williams Lake, and they had heard the team was not only good, but tough. Steven and his teammates entered the dressing room feeling nervous and unsure.

West Van knew they were in trouble the minute the puck hit the ice. At the end of the first period they were down by two and, at the end of the second, down by four. But West Van never gave up. They held their positions and made some great passes — but they just couldn't break through their opponents' defence. With four minutes to go at the end of the third period, Williams Lake was leading seven to zero. West Van was frantic and on the attack.

Will carried the puck into his zone. A big burly defenceman's breath was hot on his face, his stick slapping at the puck. Will pushed it to Josh, who lost control. The puck flew out to Steven, just inside the blueline. No one was free. In one split second he heard Jeff's words in his head: 'Shoot to score.' A small ratty player was skating hard towards him. Steven knew it was a long shot, but he swung his stick back and with all the power in his wrists he let it fly, hard and low. The puck whizzed through the screened goalie and into the net.

The team leapt around as if they had scored the tying goal. It was awesome. As Steven came through the boards onto the bench, Coach Carter slapped him on the back.

"Great shot, Meatball. You've been working hard out there. Way to go!" Steven's pride flushed his cheeks. Meatball! he noted. He liked the sound of that.

Back on the ice, with thirty seconds left, Steven chased the puck behind the net, bringing it around with a slick pass to Sizzler. Sizzler dropped it back to Steven, whose new nickname echoed in his ears. His heart was racing. He crossed over centre and just kept going. He banked it off the boards, flew past the defenceman and cut to the net. He saw the opening over the goalie's right shoulder and whipped the puck toward it. The puck hit the crossbar and dropped in front. Steven fought for the rebound and pushed it into the net. The West Van fans roared. Steven leapt into the air and his teammates rushed over to congratulate him. The final score was seven to two for Williams Lake, but Steven had scored West Van's only goals.

* * *

In the dressing room, Coach Carter gathered the team together. "You played well out there so don't let the score put
you under a spell. Just keep shooting away and eventually the
puck will start going in." He turned and looked straight at
Steven. "Great play out there, Meatball. I knew you had the
talent — you just needed a little push."

"Thanks."

Steven noticed that Josh was the only one looking down at
the floor instead of at Carter.

"It was a great pass from Josh," he suddenly found himself saying.

"Yeah? Well, maybe this afternoon the offence will get
some goals. But right now, it's breakfast on me. Let's find a
restaurant."

* * *

Back at the hotel, two hours later, the guys were busting for
fun. They had six hours until their next game and they were
ready to enjoy the hotel. As soon as he saw the steam rising
out of the outdoor pool and hot tub, Steven knew what was
first.

"To the hot tub!" he ordered, and the others agreed.

The cold snow oozed up between Steven's toes as he
hopped and yelped his way into the tub. He stretched back in
a tent of steam, mesmerized by soft white flakes swirling
down from the sky and disappearing as soon as they hit the
warm air. The hot water massaged his tired muscles and he
felt himself loosen and relax.

Everyone joined Steven in the tub. Shogo, Sizzler, Amar
and Andrew sat up around the edge. Even though they were

out of the water they were still enveloped in steam and toasty warm.

Steven shrieked as a huge snowball hit his head and exploded all over him. A war cry came at them through the steam. Shogo and Andrew dropped into the tub to duck from the flying missiles.

Josh had slipped away and, because of the dampness from the steam, was able to form the powdery snow into balls. He was swiftly knocking off the defencemen. "Offence, how about a backup," he ordered.

With that, everyone leapt out of the hot tub and dove into the pool. Scooping up the snow from around the edges, both sides tried to whip the balls before their target could dive under the water. Steven seemed to be getting pummeled from all directions but his main attacker was Josh. His snowballs seemed to be harder and faster than the others and Steven was having a hard time reaching the side of the pool to get his own ammunition. Thank goodness for Shogo, he thought, who was right at his side, blocking shots and firing them back.

Finally the snow near the edge was gone and they had to get out of the pool to find it. Steven had had enough. He streaked into the hotel, but not before Josh fired one last ball. It hit him in the middle of his back. It was pure ice.

* * *

Once changed, Steven, Will, and Sizzler headed out of the hotel, through the mini mall, in the direction of the bowling alley. On the way they passed a variety store. Inside was a row of clear bins filled with every type of candy that Steven could imagine. Amar was already inside filling a large bag. Steven dove in for one dollar's worth and was pleased with the deal.

"There's the joke shop," Steven said excitedly as he pointed to the other side of the mall.

Sizzler followed as they were all drawn into the store like magic. The boys wanted to look everywhere at once. Witches with green hair and pigs with shrivelled pink noses stared down at them from the walls. They peered into a glass case filled with fake dog poop, vomit and patches of blood oozing in different shapes and sizes. Shelves were lined with boxes of items marked 'fart gas,' 'bomb bags' and 'stink bombs.'

Steven snickered as he pictured Jeff. Payback time, he thought. Steven wanted to load up with stuff but he only had enough money to buy one can of fart gas. He brought out his wallet and fingered the money that his mum had given him to buy food throughout the weekend. He could say he'd spent it and he knew she would give him more. Thoughts of the ten dollar bill folded into squares nagged at the back of his head and he pulled out his own money, just enough for the gas.

They finally made it to the bowling alley and were assigned the lane right next to Josh and Andrew. "Who's winning?" Will asked.

The smirk that spread across Josh's face gave them the answer right away.

"Hey, Edwards, I'll bet you can't get past 100. I've got three strikes in a row. Just try and match that."

Steven felt his body tighten and anger push at his temples.

Will saw the reaction and stepped in. "Let him be, he's just being a jerk."

"Geez. Why did I try to stick up for him at the game this morning?" Steven asked his friend.

Josh overheard. His pale green eyes went hard and cold and his face flushed. "Hey, man, I don't need any help from you."

"No? So why are you always picking on me? Acting tough to impress your dad?" Suddenly, it clicked in Steven's head. That's it, he thought. He's trying to be tough, to prove he's good. He thinks his father likes Andrew better.

Steven knew what that felt like. He always thought that his dad favoured Jeff because he was so good at sports. It was funny, though, because Josh was stronger and faster than Andrew. It was obvious that Josh was the better athlete. Coach Carter did seem to favour Andrew, though, Steven reasoned. Maybe it was because he was often sick.

"Hey, jackass, I don't act tough, I am tough. Now, let's see if your bowling is any better than your hockey," Josh challenged.

"Speaking of donkeys, there seems to be a bad odour around here," said Will.

Sizzler burst into a squeaky imitation, "Ee-aw, ee-aw."

For a minute Steven had seen Josh differently, but after that comment he felt his anger returning.

"You're up," called Will. "Knock 'em dead."

Steven tried to forget about Josh. He picked up a ball from the return run and walked to the centre of the runway. The ball was hard and cold and Steven, who was a good bowler, loved the smoothness of it. He held it in front of himself and looked down the lane at the five pins. He drew his hand back, took a few steps forward and then let ball roll off his fingers. There was a thud as it made contact with the wooden floor. He followed the ball with his eyes until it crashed into the pins and sent them flying. The sound echoed through the whole alley. A strike! Yes!

Steven couldn't help but glance toward the lane next to him, but Josh was conveniently not watching. He was giving Andrew instructions on how to get a strike.

At the end of the game the boys were taking off the rented shoes when Josh came over. He didn't say anything, he just stepped in front of Steven and leaned over the score sheet.

Sizzler winked at Steven. "Speaking of bad odours," he said.

Steven immediately picked up on the clue. He reached into his pocket and, pointing at Josh's backside, he let the fart spray rip. Immediately, a warm pungent smell, worse than any outhouse, surrounded Josh and spread into the warm stale air of the bowling alley. The boys all grabbed their noses and began to gag. The squeals and sputtering mixed with hilarious laughter alerted the manager, who came charging over. All the boys dropped their shoes and ran for the stairs.

"Don't come back, you little creeps!" the manager shouted after them.

Not wanting to look back, they raced, bumping and dodging the people in the mall, until they were back in the hotel and dispersed to their own rooms.

Steven flicked on the TV and then collapsed onto his bed, still laughing.

"That was wicked." he said out loud. "Josh didn't know what hit him. I hope he has another pair of pants to wear to the banquet tonight."

Steven's thoughts lingered on Josh. He remembered watching him as he was showing Andrew how to bowl. In some ways, Josh reminded him of Jeff. He was strong, a good athlete and a bully. Steven wished Jeff could have seen his goal earlier that morning. He pictured it again in his mind and the rush quivered through him all over again. It was great, he thought, but I would really have a chance to score some goals if I could play forward this afternoon. Steven knew Carter would never let him. He had asked too many times over the season. His thoughts were drifting into one another and before he knew it he was asleep.

* * *

Down in the lobby the team was gathering to drive off to their third game of the tournament. When Steven and Will joined them, Amar and Josh were huddled together and Steven had the feeling that something was going on. Now was not the time to worry about Josh, he told himself. Now was the time to think about hockey and their next opponent, Penticton.

In the dressing room, twenty minutes later, Steven couldn't believe what Coach Carter was saying. "Okay, Meatball, you've been after me all month to let you play forward and after those two great goals this morning, you've earned your chance. I want you to play right wing with Josh at centre and Will on the left to make the first line. I think we've got a chance against these guys, so just let it rip. Andrew, you're in goal." His powerful glance moved from one boy to the next, lingering on Sizzler for a moment. "Glad to see you're with us, Bacon. What colour are we today?"

Sizzler called out in army style, "Green, sir."

* * *

Steven felt the power of his blades as he cut through the ice to take his position as right-winger. He looked across to Will. This was awesome! The puck dropped and Josh whipped it over to his friend. Will carried it across the blueline and Steven followed along the boards. Josh cruised by and received the pass, but couldn't get a shot. He took it behind the boards and slapped it over to Steven. Penticton was there at every move but just one second too slow. Will sped in front of the net to receive the pass from Steven and flipped it into the top corner of the net. West Van was on the scoreboard.

Penticton scored at the beginning of the second period and the game was tied one all. The first line offence was working well and Carter was giving them lots of ice time. The play was in Penticton's end. Josh lost the face-off but Sizzler recovered the puck and, with green strands flying from beneath his helmet, he fired the puck back to Josh. Josh took it behind the net and, zipping around the corner, tucked a wrap-around neatly into the goal. Penticton's defender lunged at him too late and they both crashed down into the goalie. Near the end of the period, Penticton's only girl scored on a breakaway and the game was tied again at two all.

"Keep the pressure on. Let them feel it," Carter coached between periods. "You can wear them down. You can beat this team."

Every muscle was tense, and his breathing was hard as Steven crouched over, his stick poised, ready to receive. This was his chance. He had to score. Suddenly, he had the puck and was tearing down the ice. He over-skated, lost the puck, but Will was right behind him to recover it. Penticton was pressing hard on Will. Steven kept skating fast toward the net. Will, with his quick moves, deked around his check and made a clean pass to Steven who torpedoed the puck into the net.

Will was the first one to crush Steven with the team hug. "Way to go, buddy! Now it's my turn," he promised.

True to his word, it took Will only two minutes before he took a clean pass from Josh, out-manoeuvred Penticton's defence, and scored to make the score four to two for West Van.

It was the last minute of play. Sizzler and Amar were holding back, running out the clock. Steven wanted the puck. He wanted one last shot. He slapped his stick on the ice. Amar flicked it over, but his shot went wide. No! Steven cried to himself. Sizzler picked it up and back-handed it into the net.

What a game! Steven thought.

9

A Stinky Situation

This was the best day Steven had ever had and it just kept going. Now they were heading off to the banquet and who knew what else would happen, Steven wondered. Half the team was crowded into Mr. Bacon's van as it slowly moved through the freshly falling snow. The flakes were so big and coming down so fast that the windshield was only clear for a second before it was covered again. Kelowna's city lights reflected off the snow crystals and the evening was all alight and sparkling.

The boys were dropped off, since the banquet was only for the players and coaches. Inside, the hall tables were set for twelve and three players from each team were to sit at every table. There were separate tables for the forwards, the defence, and the goalies. Steven and Will grabbed two seats close to the back door at a table for the offence. Just before the dinner was to start, Josh came and sat down beside Will, one seat away from Steven. He leaned in front of Will and spoke to Steven.

"Aren't you supposed to be at a defence table?"

"In case you've forgotten, tough guy, I was on your line today," Steven said, trying to keep calm. He thought back to the game. Steven, Will and Josh had actually played well together and it had felt great. So why was Josh still being a jerk? he wondered.

As though Josh could read Steven's thoughts, he said, "Oh, yeah. By the way, nice goals."

Steven looked at Will, surprised and speechless at what he had just heard. Josh was saying something nice to him!

Will answered for him, "You played well yourself. That was a sweet goal in the second period."

Lasagna dinners were served and the boys dug in ravenously. Steven loved lasagna. However, after a few bites, he pulled a face at Will, who had also slowed down.

"This is disgusting. It tastes like dung and there's no meat." Steven poked at some big chunks of onion. "Look, there's spinach in here and the pasta is like old rubber bands."

"Even slugs taste better than this," Josh added.

"Yeah." Steven couldn't help laughing. "Will, remember that survival hike we went on in grade five? We ate slugs. You're right, Josh, they did taste better."

Steven and Will started to tell the guys across from them how their whole class had gone on a survival hike and how they had caught and cooked the slugs, when Eric came up behind Josh.

"Hey, Amar says you and he went shopping this afternoon."

"Yeah. what about it?" Josh looked guarded.

"Well, I got the big number ten from Winfield sitting across from me — you know, the nasty, mouthy one? Well, he's kinda stinky and I thought we should make him smell better. What do you think?"

"I had a different target in mind," Josh said, leaning in to look down the table at Steven. "But this sounds interesting."

Josh sauntered around the tables until he reached the one where the Winfield centre was sitting. He clutched the can down by his side and, as he walked behind the big player, he pushed the button, releasing a fine spray all down his back.

The disgusting odour immediately enveloped number ten. The other players gasped as the stink spread to them.

Eric, who was back sitting across the table, grabbed his nose. "Ugh. It seems like the animal should have stayed in the barn."

The centre let out an angry growl, pushed his chair back and stood up. Even without all his gear, he looked huge. His eyes quickly scanned the room and landed on Josh heading for the back door. He took off in pursuit.

Steven and Will had been watching from their table and were doubled over laughing when they realized that Josh might need help. They rushed outside to see Josh being pushed into a snowbank at the side of the parking lot. The Winfield player grabbed Josh's hair and began pounding his head into the snow. Steven and Will charged at him from behind, knocking him off their teammate. All four of them were struggling to get up when Shogo, Sizzler and Amar appeared, bombarding the centre with huge puffs of snow. Six Winfield guys appeared and the parking lot turned into a war zone. Chunks of snow were hurled through the air and guys tried desperately to stay afoot on the slippery ground.

Coach Carter's guttural voice bellowed into the night air. "Boys! Back inside. Now!"

Will and Steven were caught off guard and were suddenly hit by an island of snow which smashed against Steven's head, covering them both.

"That's enough. The fight's over," the coach ordered.

Brushing themselves off, both teams slowly retreated to finish their now cold and definitely disgusting lasagna.

Following the dinner, each coach gave a little talk about their team and then the boys were driven back to the hotel around nine-thirty. Carter joined the parents who had gone to a nearby restaurant.

In the team room the boys were reminiscing.

"The look on that animal's face makes Gino Odjick look like a pussycat," Will laughed.

Josh grinned. "Good thing you guys showed up outside. I thought I was dead meat."

Steven couldn't resist. "The thought did occur to me to let you die, but it was even more fun decking that creep."

"Yeah?" Josh came back, "You're just lucky that Eric here put me up to it, 'cause that fart gas was meant for *you*."

Andrew, who hadn't said too much up until now, asked, "So what else did you and Amar buy?"

Amar pulled out some cards, a package of plastic ice cubes with bugs inside, a bag of little firecrackers that pop-off when you throw them onto the ground, another can of fart gas, and four bomb bags.

"Amar." Josh looked around to see if anyone was listening. "What do you say we put some of this stuff to good use?"

"Doing what?" Amar asked.

"Yeah," Steven laughed, making his voice all deep and gravelly. "Let's bomb the bar!"

"All right!" Will joined in.

"No way," said Andrew, "Dad will kill us."

"Not if you throw the bomb," Josh said to his brother. "When was the last time Dad ever yelled at you?"

Amar's dark eyes looked concerned.

"It's okay, we'll use my stuff," Josh offered. "But we've all got to be in this together."

Steven was alarmed. "Hey, I was only kidding. I don't know whether this is such a great idea."

"Oh man, don't wuss out now. It'll be awesome. Just one bomb before bed."

Everyone cracked up at the risky idea. The thought of being the thrower seemed to grow on Andrew.

"You guys have got to cover me," he warned.

"Don't worry, bro. We'll all be there. Now, is everybody in?" Josh challenged.

They all nodded and followed Josh out of the room.

It was ten o'clock and, being a Saturday night, the bar was packed. Josh, Steven, Will and Andrew crouched down, hidden in a forest of large indoor plants that separated the bar from the lobby. Shogo stood outside the hotel's souvenir shop, pretending to look at cards and magazines. Sizzler watched the main entrance to make sure none of the parents were returning. The rest of the team sat in the big sofas in front of the fire. They were close enough to see but still able to escape if something went wrong.

Steven knew they shouldn't be doing this but he couldn't back out now. The plan was that Andrew would throw the bomb and then go straight into the men's room. Sizzler would still hang by the desk and let Josh, Steven and Will know when the coast was clear to follow. The others would slowly make their way back to the team room.

"Now," Josh gave Andrew the signal to go.

Andrew looked at the three boys, nodded and then started walking slowly into the lounge. No one paid any attention to him as he reached into the top of the bomb bag and broke the little bubble. His arm came up, and he threw the bag as hard as he could. Turning, he fled without waiting to hear the bang or see the vinegar and baking soda concoction fly out in all directions. A rotten gas smell oozed out from the bag. Before anyone knew what happened he had left the lounge area and ducked into the washroom.

"Phew!" a man yelled out. "What the …?"

Others gagged, wrinkled their noses in disgust, and looked around to see what had caused the stench. One lady stood up gasping and ran from the bar. Josh, Steven and Will slapped their hands over their mouths. Hidden by the plants, they crouched down and watched the commotion. The waiter ran over to where the bomb had landed. For a moment, he looked up, searching for the culprits, and then tried to settle everyone down. The manager arrived and stood in the entrance talking with the bartender as they both looked around.

Steven's knees screamed out in pain as he held onto Will and Josh, afraid to move, afraid to breathe, his heart thudding in his chest. He noticed that the guys in the sofas had left right away and were soon followed by Shogo. The only one left in the lobby was Sizzler, who was pretending to be talking on the pay phone.

The minutes passed like hours. Feeling trapped, they waited, hoping for a moment when they could escape to join Andrew, whom Steven assumed was still in the washroom.

Just when Steven thought he was going to crack, he saw Shogo walk back into the lobby. He walked right up to the manager and said something. The manager nodded his head and went behind the desk and into his office. Sizzler looked toward the boys and made a signal for them to run.

Steven, Will and Josh scampered into the washroom. They found Andrew washing his hands.

"What took you guys so long? Every time I hear someone coming I have to wash my hands!" he said, grabbing some paper towels. "What happened?" he screeched.

"Bull's eye!" Josh slapped him on the back.

The boys doubled over laughing, then they all began at once. They could hardly speak and their words tumbled over each other. "You should have seen their faces ... some lady screamed ... the smell was wicked ... the manager is hopping mad."

Finally, Josh gained control. "We'd better hang low for a bit. Give him a few more minutes to calm down and make sure we have a safe getaway."

Steven was impatient. He wouldn't feel safe until he was in the team room with the others. "I wonder what Shogo said to the manager."

Will sat on the bathroom counter swinging his legs nervously. "I don't know, but I hope he got him laughing."

Josh opened the door a crack and searched for Sizzler. He spotted him, still pretending to talk on the phone. Sizzler saw Josh and shook his head. Josh retreated. A few moments later, he tried again. He could see the manager at the desk.

The boys were getting antsy. They wanted to get out of there. Steven went to the door. He opened it just a sliver so that he could see Sizzler and the desk. "As soon as I say go, we're outa here." He waited a few more minutes. "Oh no!" he moaned.

"What is it?" Josh demanded. "What's happening?"

"The manager's talking to Sizzler. He's pointing over here. He's got Sizzler by the arm and they're coming this way!" Steven let the door close and immediately looked around for an escape.

The boys stared at each other, struck with panic. There was nowhere to go. Andrew started to whimper.

"Don't worry, Andrew," Josh tried to comfort his brother. "Just stick to our story. Remember, Dad never gets mad at you. This guy can't do anything to us."

"He could kick us out of the hotel," Will said nervously.

"He's not going to do that. Look, just stay calm," Josh instructed them.

The door opened and Sizzler entered with a look of anguish and apology on his face. The manager stood tall behind him, still holding onto Sizzler's arm. Sarcasm dripped from his angry words, "Are these friends of yours?"

"Yes, sir."

"Having a little fun, were we?" he asked, looking at each boy with piercing eyes. No one spoke, so he continued. "I don't appreciate this kind of behaviour in my hotel. Where is your coach?"

Josh spoke up, "At a restaurant, sir. He should be back shortly."

"Well, you can just sit down in the lobby until he comes back." Opening the door, he nodded his head in the direction of the big sofas. "No one is to move. Understand?"

The boys all nodded. They left the washroom and sat down to wait.

Coach Carter arrived at 10:45 p.m. He immediately noticed the boys and looked at his watch. He could tell from the looks on their faces that something was wrong. As he approached, so did the manager.

"What's going on here?" Carter asked him apprehensively.

"It seems your boys felt the need to cause some havoc." The manager quickly explained what had happened. "I don't need to tell you, Mr. Carter, that this is not the kind of behaviour I expected from your team."

"No, it's absolutely unacceptable," Carter said calmly, but fury burned from every tightened muscle in his face. "If you don't mind, I'd like to deal with this myself. I can assure you it will be well taken care of."

To Steven, the manager suddenly looked meek in comparison to Coach Carter.

"Good. I'll leave you to it." He turned, and without another word he walked away.

Steven's throat felt parched and tight. He could hear his heart beat in his ears and he felt sick to his stomach. In the last fifteen minutes he had chewed all of his nails and now he was working on the skin.

When the coach began to speak his voice was gruff. "Who threw the bomb?"

Andrew didn't hesitate. "I did."

The coach's shock was obvious. "Who's idea was it?"

"Mine," Andrew answered, before the rest of them had a chance. Steven was amazed. It was almost as if Andrew was enjoying it. Steven himself was so nervous he continued to feel sick.

"Josh didn't put you up to this?"

"No, sir."

"Where did you get the bomb?"

"I bought it at the joke shop."

Carter turned to Josh. "So, what was your part in this little adventure?"

Josh hesitated for a moment, "I was on guard."

"Steven," Carter said suddenly, "Did you think this was a good idea?"

Steven looked at the others, not knowing what to say. "I did at the beginning, but I don't now."

"Will, I would have thought you would have used your brains." Will hung his head. "You, Edwards and Bacon, go to your rooms. I want to chat a little more with my sons and I'll come to see you when I've finished." The coach paused for a second. When no one moved, he shouted, "Now!" The three boys jumped up and hurried off.

"Let's stop in at the team room," Steven suggested. "We should let everyone know what's happened."

"What do you think he'll do? Do you think he'll send us home?" Will sounded worried and depressed "How could we do such a ridiculous thing? How did we think we could get away with it?"

"It was my stupid idea," Steven moaned. "Just when the coach is starting to like me I go and blow it. It seems like I'm always blowing it. There goes my hockey career."

When they got to the team room no one was there so they continued slowly down the hall. Steven and Will had to go past the Carters' room to get to their own rooms. They started to sprint past but paused when they heard voices. To their surprise, it was Andrew and Josh yelling at each other.

Andrew sounded tearful, "It was my idea. Nobody made me do it. I wanted to do it."

Josh screamed back, "I was the one who bought the stuff with Amar. It was my idea."

"It was not."

"It was so."

"Stop!" Coach Carter's voice boomed out. "It seems to me you are both to blame. I'm going to talk to the others and I want you two in bed."

Steven and Will bolted from the door and raced down the hall to Steven's room. Steven didn't even have a chance to turn on his TV when he heard the knock.

With a swish of his hand, Carter indicated that the boys should sit on the edge of the bed. He pulled up a chair.

"I don't need to tell you how disappointed I am in you. We trusted you to behave and you have disgraced our team."

The coach leaned forward and his strong hands gripped his thighs. He looked powerful and mad. "What do you have to say for yourselves?"

"Sorry," Steven and Will mumbled together, hanging their heads.

"Sorry? Not enough," Carter said, raising his voice.

Steven met his eyes. He wanted to lie, to agree that it was Andrew, to let him take the fall. He struggled with the words forming in his mouth. "It was my idea," he choked out.

"Not you too?" the coach sounded exasperated.

"No, it was me, really. It was my idea to bomb the bar. Josh had the stuff but it was my idea." Steven held his breath, waiting for what was to come.

"As far as I'm concerned you're all in this together. Your behaviour tonight was inexcusable. You're a total disgrace and an embarrassment to your team, to your parents and to me." The coach stood up.

"I'm going to bed," he said in a disgusted tone. "I'll see you, eight o'clock sharp, in the team room. I suggest you both think about what disciplinary action is in order. Will, go back to your room." With that, he turned and left.

In bed minutes later, Steven's thoughts were banging about in his head and his stomach was twisted and tight. He didn't know what was going to happen the next day, but he was glad he had told the truth. He fell into a much-needed but unsettled sleep.

10

A Chance for Colorado

The coach stepped into the team room the following morning and the only sound to be heard was the hum of the television. The table with juice, bananas and muffins had hardly been touched. He walked over to the TV and flicked it off. All eyes were on him. For a few moments he stared back at the boys, letting the silence hang in the air.

"By now you all know what took place last night. I realize that you may have not all been involved, but we are a team and so this act has hurt the whole team. It threw a disgraceful reflection on each and every one of you — on your team, your parents and on me. What are we going to do about it?"

The boys looked at each other and at the floor, anywhere but at Carter. Finally, Steven's voice cracked out nervously. "I think we should apologize to the manager."

"That's a good start, Edwards."

Will added, "Could we write a letter and all sign it and give it to him?"

Carter thought for a moment. "What about the people in the bar?"

"Well," Steven continued, "we could apologize to the bartender and he could post a letter in the bar." The boys all nodded in agreement.

"Right," Carter said, looking at his watch. "You have one hour before we have to leave for our final game against Vernon."

He reached into his folder and pulled out some paper. "Will, as captain, you can write the letter. The boys can tell you what to write. I will be back in thirty minutes for the good copies, one for the manager and one for the bar, signed by all and ready to be delivered along with a personal apology by Josh, Andrew, Will and Steven. You will all explain to your parents what took place and your part in the activity. I would disband the team but we have all worked too hard to do that. However, if anything like this happens again I will not hesitate. One last thing. I don't *ever* want to see or smell anything that resembles a stink bomb — here or anywhere."

                                    * * *

In the dressing room two hours later, it was as if nothing had happened. The smell of stale sweat, the sound of velcro ripping and of lockers slamming was all the same, and the playful chatter carried on. It was only after the coach entered the room that the mood seemed to change.

"Meatball, you're back on defence. Shogo, you're in goal. Let's play hockey."

That was it. He turned and left.

Steven felt bad. The whole team felt bad. Standing up, he declared, "Let's win this one for Carter."

"Yes!" Will shouted, throwing his fist in the air. "For Carter."

The rest copied. "For Carter," they echoed, and followed Steven out onto the ice.

As the game started, Steven found himself sitting on the bench with Josh and Will. Andrew was there, too. They watched as Eric snared the puck and passed it to the left-winger who flew down the ice. Vernon's defender tripped him with his stick and Eric went flying.

Sizzler recovered the puck but a Vernon man was right on him. "We *heard* you had a girl on your team. Where do you get your hair done?"

Sizzler didn't flinch. He barged past him, took a shot and scored.

Steven came onto the ice and took his position with Amar. Vernon got control and brought the puck into West Van's zone. Steven stole the puck but a nasty winger came at him, slashing his wrists. Steven lost control but the winger kept at him and slammed him up against the boards. Steven hit the ice feeling like he'd never move again.

Will took advantage of the power play and, with his fast skating and quick moves, he scored two goals in two minutes. Steven banged him on his head in victory.

"Their skating is as trashy as their talk," Will joked loudly. "That makes them losers!"

On the bench, Carter was quiet. This made the boys work even harder. Every time Steven was on the ice he worked his butt off. He warded off the elbows and the tripping but when the referee wasn't looking he gave it right back. Every time the puck was in West Van's end he was there, right in front of their goal, blocking, taking it back, shooting it down the ice. Nothing was going to get by him and nothing did.

By the beginning of the third period all the bashing was beginning to wear on Steven. The referees weren't calling the penalties and they seemed to favour Vernon. Steven's wrists ached. The whole team was slowing down, getting sloppy. Vernon got back into the game with two cheap goals.

The clock showed one minute to go. The score was three to two for West Van. Steven was just inside the blueline when the puck came out. He looked to pass it to Will or Josh but they were hounded by Vernon's defence. Steven pulled back his stick. He winced in pain but slapped a shot through a gap and into the net. The winger charged him from behind and

Steven kissed the ice. That was too much for Josh who flew at the winger with his fists flying. The referees charged in to pull them apart. Vernon's player got a major penalty and had to leave the rink. Josh got two minutes for fighting.

At the end of the game the scoreboard flashed a final score of four to two for West Van.

In the dressing room, everyone was whooping and jumping about when Carter came in.

"Nice game out there boys," he said, with a passive tone which surprised Steven. "Your defence was great and I saw some good passing." Carter's words were there but there was no feeling behind them. He seemed distant and his shoulders were slumped.

Steven wanted the old coach back, the one that yelled and screamed, the one for whom hockey was a passion. They had won and he should be ecstatic! Steven thought. But he wasn't and Steven knew why. They had let him down — Steven had let him down.

* * *

Later on in the day, as Mrs. Edwards drove the van toward the summit of the Coquihalla Highway, Steven thought about the games, the goals he had scored and how well he had played. He felt good about himself and wished his dad could have been there to see him. What a hoot they had had. He chuckled out loud.

Will looked up from his comic. "What are you laughing about?"

Steven laughed again. "I was thinking about the bombing. Did you see the look on that lady's face? She didn't know what had hit her."

Will laughed with him. "It was so sweet! You know, I thought we were dead meat. I thought Carter was going to cut us up into little pieces and throw us to the Ogopogo."

"Me too," Steven agreed. Everyone knew about the legend of the monster that lived in Okanagan Lake.

Steven thought about how downtrodden Carter had looked after the game. "I guess he's not such a bad guy. I mean, look how much we've all improved. I used to think he hated me but now I realize he actually believed in me. Just like he believes in Josh and Andrew. He yells to make us work harder. I think he is a great coach."

"Yeah, the discipline has done us all some good."

"You know, I can't believe I'm saying this, but Josh isn't so bad either. He seems to have this hang-up about his dad liking Andrew better, but I can understand that. I know how he feels. I think I'm beginning to like him."

Will jumped in, "Could you believe Andrew? I thought I was going to choke when he calmly said he had done it. He didn't flinch. Boy, I tell ya, that has got to take guts."

"Yeah," Steven agreed.

"What a weekend!" Will laughed. "What a great bunch of guys."

* * *

The next week West Van played North Van, their main rivals, and beat them six to zero. Carter was back to his old self but there was something different about the team. It was as though they had suddenly clicked and come together. Josh was still yapping off at Steven but somehow the tone was more playful and Steven didn't take offence but shot the comments right back. Steven had always preferred Shogo to be in goal but now he was happy with both their goalies. Amar had been practising a lot and his skating had really improved.

Will was scoring more goals than ever and even Josh had come out of his slump.

On the way home in the car Steven beamed with pleasure as his father talked on and on about how well the team had played and how much it had improved.

"Steven, you have worked hard and it shows."

"Thanks, Dad."

"I was talking to Coach Linden after his practice with the rep team. He's short a defender and asked if you'd like to play with his team in Colorado. It may put you in a good position when trying out for the rep team next year."

Steven couldn't believe what he was hearing. Colorado! Playing for the rep team! he thought excitedly. His insides were bouncing around and he could hardly sit still. "Thanks, Dad!"

"Don't thank me, you've earned it." Mr. Edwards turned to his son with a smile, "It was Coach Linden's suggestion. He's seen you play and he thinks you've got some talent. Now it's up to you to prove that he's right."

Steven's happiness filled the car. He couldn't wait to get home to tell Jeff. He, Steven Edwards, was going to play on the rep team, he beamed to himself. He couldn't wait to phone Will.

* * *

Steven knew Will's phone number as well as his own. Pick up, pick up, pick up, he thought impatiently as the ringing echoed in his ear.

"Will, you'll never guess."

"So then I won't bother. What's up?"

Steven blurted out his news with cocky pleasure. "I'm going to Colorado and I get to play with the peewee rep team in their tournament."

"Yeah? That's great! When is it?"

"The third week in February."

There was an awkward silence on the other end of the phone.

"Will, are you there?"

"Yeah, yeah, I'm here." Another silence. "Steve, that's when our playoffs are."

Steven shook his head. "No, they're the next week," he said in disbelief.

"I've got the schedule right here. The finals are in the last week of February but the playoffs are when the rep team is in Colorado."

"*Noooo.*" Steven's voice was filled with anguish.

"Tough luck, pal." Will said, trying to be sympathetic. "We need you. You can't desert us."

Steven said goodbye and slammed down the phone.

"What's the matter, bro?" Jeff asked, giving Steven a playful punch to his shoulder.

Steven slammed his fist on the counter. The toaster jumped. "No, no, no!" he said, pounding his fist with each word. "I don't care. I'm going anyway. I'll just have to miss the playoffs. Can you believe it?" he said turning to his brother. "The playoffs are during the same week as Colorado."

11

Left Behind

Steven sat watching Jeff pack. He stared into the suitcase and his disappointment filled the room. Jeff silently pulled clothes from his drawers, haphazardly folding them and shoving them into his bag. To break the silence he slipped a CD into his ghetto blaster, but Steven wasn't interested in the music.

"Dad said I could go," Steven said.

"I know, bro. This is what you've been hoping for all year."

"Now I can't. And the worst part — it was my decision. And it's just the playoffs. We could lose and then I will have missed the trip for nothing."

Jeff stopped folding and a brightness came over his face. "You could change your mind. You could still come."

"No," Steven shook his head. He knew he couldn't let his team down. Ever since Kelowna they were all playing well. It felt awesome to be part of the team. He had a new respect for his coach and he didn't want to let him down again. No, Steven thought, he knew he had made the right decision but he wished Colorado and the playoffs didn't have to be during the same week. It just wasn't fair.

"Steven, Jeff, dinner's ready," their mother called.

"What are we having?" Steven asked, as he left Jeff's room and entered the kitchen.

"Chili — one of your favourites," Mrs. Edwards replied, smiling gently.

Jeff dipped one shoulder down to bodycheck Steven up against the fridge. "He only likes chili because it gives him gas. As if he needs any more hot stinky air than he already has."

The boys' mum pulled a face. "That's enough, Jeff."

Steven poked around in his dinner. "This looks like one of your yucky vegetarian dishes," he complained.

"There's no meat in it, Steven, if that's what you mean."

"Where's Dad? You wouldn't be serving this to him."

Mrs. Edwards sighed and got up from the table. "Your dad's working late, and yes I would serve this to him. I'm going to a meeting. Please clean up when you're done."

Steven stayed at the table, leaning on one elbow. He couldn't eat another bite. He got up and took his big chili mug to the counter. He couldn't throw it into the garbage because his mum would see it. He saw the plastic bag container, the one that hung like a sausage beside the fridge, and got an idea.

Steven pulled out a grocery bag, dumped his chili into it, tied a knot and took it out onto the back porch where a light drizzle felt good against the rage he felt inside. He pulled his arm back, twirled the bag around his head like a lasso and let the chili go, intending it to fly out into the back of the garden. Whoosh. The bag burst in mid air, exploding chili all over the deck.

"Oh, great," Steven cried. "What a mess! It's a good thing it's raining." Back inside, he turned on the TV and sunk into the sofa.

* * *

The next morning, Steven waved as his dad and Jeff drove off to the airport. His dad gave him a big hug and wished him well in the playoffs. He said he was proud of him for making the right decision and he was sure they would do well. Steven went back into the house feeling better. After all, he was going to have a week without his brother always beating on him and telling him he was a wuss. Still sleepy, he shuffled his way into the kitchen, only to find his mother in a very angry state. Her hands were burrowing into her hips and her angry glare startled him.

"What's the matter?" he asked innocently.

"Come with me, young man," she said, grabbing him by the elbow and directing him outside onto the back porch.

As soon as Steven saw the early morning sun bouncing off the outside of the house, he knew what the problem was. Deep blotches of dark red and brown were splattered in an arc about three feet long across the white stucco.

"What happened?" he asked, without much conviction. To himself, he thought, geez, I hadn't noticed that it got on the house too.

"That's what I would like you to tell *me*," his mother said accusingly.

Steven hated it when his mother was cross with him.

"It wasn't me. I just got up." Then, trying to make it sound convincing, he added, "What is it?"

"You know darn well what it is."

"How would I know what it is?"

"Why don't you go and have a better look."

Steven carefully walked up to the side of the house and reached up to touch it.

"Do you think that perhaps it could be chili?" his mum asked sarcastically. "Perhaps vegetarian chili? The kind that you hate?"

"What? You think I threw my chili against the house?"

"Yes, I do."

"Well, I didn't. It must have been Jeff"

"Jeff likes chili."

"So do I."

"Come on, Steven, please tell me the truth."

"I'm telling you the truth. I didn't do it." Steven walked past his mother and back into the house. He couldn't look at her. "I've got to get going or I'll be late for school."

"Please come right home. I want this settled."

"There's nothing to settle, I didn't do it."

"Come home *immediately* after school."

"Fine."

Steven ran all the way down the hill into the school grounds. The bell had already rung and he pushed his way through the crowded hallway towards his locker.

He became aware of an extra excitement all around him. Claire and Jennifer were coming out of his room and bumped into him. Claire blushed redder that her hair ribbon.

Steven wondered what was up. Then he saw everyone milling around delivering little white envelopes to various desks. He stopped dead in his tracks. It was Valentine's Day. With so much on his mind, he'd totally forgotten.

Slipping into his desk he gathered up the envelopes, looking for one in particular. His throat went tight as he realized that the one he was looking for wasn't there. But she was just here, he told himself. Surely she would have brought one for him. Steven looked through the pile again. This day is getting worse and worse, he whispered.

Miss Drummond's voice cut into his thoughts. "All right, boys and girls. Everyone back into your own seats. Please put away your cards for now and take out your math books."

Steven reached into his desk and his hand brushed against something which fell to the floor. He bent over to pick it up and smiled when he saw the small green box with a heart painted in each corner. He quickly picked it up and held it inside his desk where he could see it but others couldn't.

Carefully, he slipped off the lid. Inside was a handmade friendship bracelet woven with red and white thread. Steven turned the box over looking for a card and there, on the bottom, drawn in the same red polish, were the initials *C.A.* Underneath was another heart and underneath the heart were his initials, *S.E.* Even the inside of the box had been painted in the shiny red. Steven attached the bracelet to his wrist. He pulled out his books and began to work on his math, but in his head he was trying to solve a different problem: What could he get for Claire?

Suddenly he knew. There was a store in Dundarave, a local shopping village that sold things from Africa — little carved elephants, zebras, spears, masks and some interesting African jewellery. Steven had ten dollars left from his allowance. Yes, he thought, he knew what he was going to do.

At lunch, Steven and Will headed down to the store. They each picked up an elephant. They tilted the brown glossy animals forward, as if in a face-off, and used their trunks as hockey sticks. Will gave the commentary.

"The fans cheer as the referee drops the puck." Fwapp, fwapp, the trunks collided.

The woman who owned the store came over with a stormy face. "May I help you?" she inquired curtly.

Will put down his elephant and gave the lady one of his most charming smiles. "Yes," he said. "My friend here is looking for a special something for his girlfriend."

Steven felt his face go bright red.

"Did you have something in mind?" she asked, turning to Steven. "The elephants are fifteen dollars. She might be happier with one of the beaded dolls which are only twelve."

Steven replaced his elephant and moved over to the glassed-in counter. Immediately, he saw what he wanted. There was a small silver ring with a single blue heart. It was perfect.

"How much is that little ring?" he asked hopefully.

The lady reached under the counter and picked up the ring. Handing it to him she said, "It's fifteen dollars."

Steven's heart sank. "I forgot it was Valentine's Day today and didn't get anything for, ah, you know," he stumbled on the words. "I want to get her something today but I only have ten dollars. This ring is perfect."

Will elbowed him gently in the ribs, encouraging him to go on.

"I don't want her to be without a Valentine." Steven looked up pleading.

"I think she's a pretty lucky girl and I don't want to be accused of impeding young love. Okay, you can have it for ten."

Suddenly, Steven heard some snickering and turned around to see Shogo and Sizzler poking their faces out from behind a rack of batik dresses.

"Oooh, impeding young love!" Sizzler mimicked.

"Thank you," Steven said, feeling self-conscious. He turned to Will and, through the side of his mouth, whispered, "Get those guys out of here."

* * *

Steven could see the red ribbon from the other end of the hall. He clutched the little box in his pocket. He felt a little sweaty and could feel his heart racing along with the words he was rehearsing in his head. He would stop and say, 'Here, this is for you.' No. 'I bought you a little something.' No. 'Claire, this is for you.'

As he came closer to her locker she turned and saw him coming. She smiled at him and a warmth rushed up into his face. His throat went dry. He pulled the box out and extended it toward her. She in turn reached to take the box.

As their hands met he mumbled, "Happy Valentine's Day," and kept on walking.

* * *

Will and Steven walked slowly up the hill. Steven was in no hurry to get home.

"Why don't you want to come over?" Will asked happily as his feet sprung off the pavement with each step. He had a Valentine from Jennifer folded and tucked carefully into his wallet. "We'll play NHL on the computer."

"I can't. I've got homework and I want to rest up for the game tonight."

"That's my line," Will laughed. "Come on, you've got all weekend to do your homework. We might learn some moves."

"Naw," Steven said, not really listening to Will, knowing he would soon have to face his mum. He knew his mum didn't believe him. Of course, it couldn't be Jeff, Mr. Perfect, Steven thought bitterly. Besides, it was her fault for making that disgusting stuff, he reasoned. He vowed to himself to never eat chili again.

By the time Steven got home he had worked himself into a state. He went straight into his room, closed the door and got out his books. Maybe if his mum saw him working she'd leave him alone.

No such luck. She came into his room and sat down on the edge of his bed.

"So, Steven. What about our problem?" The voice was calm but there was a sadness in it that Steven hated. Sometimes he wished she'd just yell at him instead of making him feel guilty. Well, he told himself, it wasn't going to work. He wasn't going to tell her. He kept staring down at his book.

"Steven, look at me." She waited until he raised his eyes and stared defiantly back at her.

"I know you did it. There is no one else who could have done it. Lying to me is worse than throwing the chili."

Steven said nothing.

"Honey," she said softly, "if you continue to lie to me I won't be able to trust you. If I can't trust you there are many things that I won't be able to let you do. I know it is hard, but if you tell me the truth it will be a lot easier on both of us."

For a minute a stubborn silence filled the room.

"Steven, do you remember at Christmas when I asked you if you'd seen the ten dollars?" Mrs. Edwards paused, waiting for an answer. "Let me help you. It was all folded up and I left it on the kitchen counter. I asked you about it just before we left for Whistler."

Steven felt himself sinking. He had thought that one was a done deal.

"Jeff told me that you liked to fold your money up into little squares. He thought that was goofy." She was just stating a fact. "So, do you, Steven? Do you like to fold your money up into little squares?"

Steven was losing this one and he knew it. He felt the anger coming at him from all directions. He was mad at his mum, mad at his brother and mad at himself.

"Okay, okay," he shouted. "I took the money. I lied to you then. I saw it there on the counter and I couldn't resist it."

There, he thought defiantly, she should be happy now that he had confessed. This should take the heat off.

"But," he added emphatically, "I didn't throw the chili."

Steven said the words but inside he was dying. It used to be so easy to lie, to see if he could get away with it, but ever since Kelowna he'd get this sick feeling. He remembered how impressed he was with Andrew when he had stood up to his dad. Steven had followed his lead and it had felt good. This lie was stuck in his throat. He wanted to get past it, but he just couldn't.

His mum sighed deeply. "Thank you. At least we have one cleared up. I'm sorry, but I still think you threw the chili. If I'm wrong I apologize. I want you to come and clean off the deck and the house. I doubt that it will come off — we'll probably have to paint the whole thing."

She stood up to leave. "You are grounded for two weeks. I am tempted to stop you from playing hockey tonight but I don't want you to let your team down. It's bad enough that you have let me down."

Mrs. Edwards reached into the pouch at the front of her apron and pulled out a package. Steven could see the red and white jellybeans and the chocolate hearts through the cellophane wrapping. She leaned over and kissed the top of his head.

"I am not happy with your behaviour but I do love you. Happy Valentine's Day," she said, without smiling, and turned and left the room.

12

The Final Play

This was it. This was the most important game of the season against North Van. West Van had beaten them twice but North Van had lost no other games and was leading the league. This is what they had worked hard for all year. Steven knew if they played well, if they won tonight, that it would set the tone for the playoffs. If they lost, it would throw a curse on them and it would be harder to bounce back. In the dressing room, the guys were tense and filled with nervous excitement.

Sizzler came flying in with his hair sticking out in all directions, a brilliant cranberry red. Shogo started crowing like a rooster and, in seconds, the whole team was squawking away.

Pleased by the reaction, Sizzler dropped his jeans to reveal a pair of boxer shorts covered in big red hearts. The squawks turned to laughter.

"These, my fellow chickens, are going to lead us to victory. And, if we win, I'm not changing them."

Steven loved it. "Hey, guys, we've got our own Dennis Rodman," he laughed.

"Pleeeeease, don't headbutt the referee," Will chipped in.

The minute their coach entered the room, however, the mood became more serious. Each player was silently fixing his own game. Each one was hoping to score a goal, make a save, and win. Who would start? Steven wondered. What would the lines be? Would it be Shogo or Andrew in goal?

Steven still thought that Shogo was the better goalie. On the other hand, Andrew had turned into an awesome goalie as well. He seemed to be stronger than he was at the beginning of the year and, though he was still smaller than Josh, they looked more alike. Even his eyes had come alive with the same aggressive instinct his brother had.

"Okay, boys," Carter began, "this is it. This is the final showdown. If you win tonight and you win tomorrow morning you're a shoo-in for the championship. It would be great, but more than anything else I want to see you playing your best hockey. I want to see some great passing and I want you all to be alert. Use your heads and play smart. Now, these guys are big, and good, but you can beat them."

"First line defence: Meatball, Bacon. First line offence: Eric at centre, Will and Josh. Andrew, you're in goal but Shogo, be ready. If you don't play tonight you'll be playing the next game. Okay team, let's play hockey!"

Steven's blades hit the ice the minute the gate closed behind the Zamboni. He felt ready. He knew what Jeff would have said to him. 'Skate hard. Don't let them past you. You've got the size, use it.' For a few seconds, Steven thought about Jeff and wished he was there watching him. He wished his father was watching, too. Then he regained his focus and told himself: We've got to win.

Eric won the face-off, passed the puck out to Will and over to Josh. North Van's defence shoved Josh into the corner boards. Josh flicked it out to Will, who cut in front of the goal. A quick shot hit the pipes and ricocheted out. North Van grabbed the puck and raced back down the ice. Steven and Sizzler kept in front, their thighs pumping hard, pushing backwards, blocking the goal. Steven stole the puck and slapped it out of North Van's end back to Will, a perfect pass.

The pace was set, each team hungry for a win, each player fighting hard for control.

Back and forth they skated as the crowd cheered. The battle was on. At the end of the first period there was still no score. West Van had twelve shots on goal, North Van had eight. Andrew had made some awesome saves and was as confident as Steven had ever seen him. He wasn't surprised when his father left him in for the second period.

With two minutes left in the second period, there was still no score. Steven was amazed as he watched Amar scramble after the puck and crash against his opponents. Suddenly the whistle blew and a penalty was given to West Van for tripping. It was the last minute of play in the period and West Van had given North Van a power play. Could they hold them back? Steven wondered.

The face-off was in North Van's end. Each boy bent over, ready. The puck dropped. Josh lost it to a North Van player, who passed it quickly to his right wing, across the net, and back to the centre, who rushed at Andrew, smacking the puck high up into the corner. Andrew reached wildly, grazing the edge of the puck and tipped it out of the goal. The buzzer blew. Still no score.

This was it. One more period. Could they hold North Van off? Steven worried. Andrew was still in goal. If he got a shutout it would be his first.

"Defence," Carter hollered. "You can hold them back, I know you can. Meatball, you're skating well but stay on them. Don't leave any holes. Bacon, let's see what that fiery hair can do for you. Offence, shoot that puck. Just keep smacking it and one's got to go in. I can feel a win in my gut. Let's go for it."

Just past the five minute mark the ref's hand went up. Another penalty was called against West Van. With shoulders down and stick dragging the player was guided towards the box. Steven and Sizzler were in a good position, right in front of the net, ready for North Van's centre who was beating down toward them. He fired a shot, Andrew took it off his shoulder, and the puck went over the glass. North Van kept control but couldn't get it past Steven. He was right there with every shot, his energy exploding inside him.

Finally they killed the power play and were back in force. North Van wouldn't let up and West Van was having trouble keeping the puck in their opponent's zone. Two more penalties against West Van, two more power plays. The clock was ticking, the fans were anxious, gasping with every save. Steven didn't let them down. North Van kept smacking. Even the defence was pressing in on Andrew. Steven stopped a shot, and quickly fed the puck out to Josh who was hanging by the boards. He raced up the side, and passed it over to Will, who crossed the blueline then fed it into Eric who was coming up the middle. North Van was fast to follow but not fast enough. Eric thundered down upon the goalie with Josh and Will on either side. He went to shoot, faked, then passed the puck to Will who slipped it into the left corner. The goalie didn't have a chance. The fans clapped wildly and West Van was on the scoreboard.

The tension in the rink mounted. The coaches were alert. In the stands, the spectators were screaming. The players were wild, desperate to win. North Van couldn't believe they were behind and they scrambled at every turn, becoming sloppy in their last desperate attempt to put West Van down. The buzzer went. West Van had won.

The boys on the bench leapt onto the ice and attached themselves to the jubilant team hug. They rushed toward the goalie and Andrew, ecstatic with his first shutout, beamed as each player banged him on the head with their big gloves.

Carter joined them on the ice and they filed past a defeated North Vancouver. He then waited at the gate. "Great game, Meatball," he said patting him on the back. "You led the defence out there. Way to go!"

The coach's words vibrated inside Steven's head. In the dressing room the cheers bounced off the ceiling and walls. Steven's spirits were flying. Punching the air in victory, he had to scream to be heard, "Yes, Yes!"

Eric pulled off his skates and suddenly leapt on Sizzler, yanking off his helmet and messing up his hair. Before Sizzler knew what was happening the team had him on the floor. They pulled off his gear until they had him down to the Valentine boxer shorts. It took five of them to hold Sizzler while Will stripped off the shorts and chucked them around to each player.

"We love these lucky pants," Will cried out.

Sizzler leapt from boy to boy, snatching at his shorts, his face as red as the big hearts, until he finally grabbed them and slipped them back on.

Steven, still bursting with the thrill of victory, was the last to leave the dressing room. Just as he was standing up to leave, his eye caught sight of a peaked hat lying under a bench. "Sweet!" he cried out, as he turned the hat over in his hand. It was the best hat he'd ever seen, with a pro back like the professionals wear. It was made out of wool with the new Philadelphia logo embedded on the front. It would have cost at least forty bucks. Slipping it onto his head, Steven looked into the mirror.

"Sweet," he repeated at his reflection.

With his face still red and his hair wet from sweat, Steven lugged his bag over his shoulder and swayed out of the dressing room to catch up with Will. Steven saw the girls before he saw anyone else and immediately he felt his face flush. Had they been there for the whole game? Claire and Jennifer were standing back watching shyly and Steven felt a wave of panic as he got closer. This girlfriend thing was new to Steven and he felt embarrassed. He turned to Will with a look crying for help. Will just bugged his eyes out and shrugged his shoulders. As Steven passed Claire and Jennifer he smiled awkwardly but kept walking toward his mum.

"Great game, Steven." Mrs. Edwards praised her son as he plunked his bag down at her feet.

"Thanks," Steven said, glancing at Will. He turned back to his mum. "We're going to get a drink in the cafeteria."

Mrs. Edwards had seen the girls too. "Sure, I'll meet you at the car in thirty minutes."

As the boys entered the cafeteria they saw Claire and Jennifer sitting at a table with their heads together sipping on a cola. Steven sucked in his breath, holding it for courage, and walked over. "Hi," he said. "Can we join you?"

"Sure," both Claire and Jennifer said at the same time.

Steven and Will got their drinks and sat down. Steven immediately noticed that Claire was wearing the silver ring with a blue heart which he gave her and he felt the colour rise to his cheeks. He was nervous. This was ridiculous! he thought. He wanted to say something but all words escaped him. How could he ask her on a date if he felt so weird just trying to talk to her? he wondered.

Claire looked at him. "Good game Steven. I sure miss being on the team."

"Does it hurt when they smash you against the boards like that?" Jen asked. "It makes an awful noise."

Steven felt relieved. Hockey was something he could talk about. "Next year, in bantam, we're allowed to bodycheck. Then you'll really hear some *real* slamming up against the boards." He looked at Will and they nodded their heads in agreement.

Claire scrunched up her face. "I liked playing hockey but I couldn't handle that."

"That's the best part of the game, the harder you hit, the better." Will carried on. "Except if they're double your size, then you might think twice about trying to wipe them out."

Will suddenly noticed Steven's hat. "Hey, cool, where'd you get the hat?"

I bought it, were the words that he wanted to say, but he hesitated and pushed back the lie. Claire was looking directly at him.

"I found it," he said slowly.

"All right! What a coup. You'd better stash it in case someone recognizes it," Will said, clearly envious.

"Naw, actually I'm going to turn it in at the front desk. If no one claims it then maybe I can keep it, but I'd be ticked off if I was the one who had lost it and no one turned it in."

Steven's confidence was up and he was feeling better and better. A part of him desperately wanted to keep the hat but he suddenly knew that what he said was right, and if it was his hat he would want it back. He looked away from Will's astonishment and glanced at Claire.

Right then and there Steven made a decision. "Claire, would you like to come to the movies with me tomorrow night?"

This time it was Claire's turn to blush. "I guess. I'll have to ask my mum."

Suddenly, there was silence in the group. Steven could tell from the look on Will's face that he wanted to say something too. Jennifer looked down into her drink. Steven flicked his head, encouraging his friend.

Will hesitated, but only for a second. "Jen," he started slowly, "would you like to go too?"

Steven jumped in, "We could go to see *Mighty Ducks III*. I hear there are some great hockey scenes."

The girls both groaned and everybody laughed.

* * *

In the car on the way home Mrs. Edwards praised her son. "That was a great game, Steven. You stopped so many shots on goal. The whole team played well!"

Steven had to agree, and it felt good. "Thanks, Mum. Did you see that last pass out to Josh?" His mum nodded. "And Eric's fake and pass over to Will? He slipped it in. He scored!" Steven's arms flew up as he relived the moment. "I can't wait to tell Jeff."

Steven thought of his brother down in Colorado and wasn't envious at all. He wouldn't have missed this game for anything. He knew his dad would have been proud of him. He had done it all by himself and as far as he was concerned, you couldn't ask for anything better.

Mrs. Edwards broke into his thoughts. "You must be starving. You hardly ate any of your pasta before the game."

"Yeah," Steven agreed. "I was too nervous to eat."

"How about a victory hamburger?"

Steven looked over at his mum and then stared out of the window. After a moment, he asked, "Have you got any more of that chili?"

Caught off guard his mum swerved her head quickly in his direction.

Steven didn't like the look on her face but his new confidence was giving him courage. "Yes, I think I'd like some chili," he paused and then squinted up his eyes and made a face as if each word he was about to say was painful. "And this time, I'll try not to get it all over the house."

Mrs. Edwards burst out, "Steven, Steven, Steven." She began shaking her head. "I was so cross with you!"

Something triggered inside Steven and he started laughing so hard he began to snort.

"I was sure the rain would have washed it away." Then, after several quiet moments, he sighed deeply and added, "I'm sorry Mum. I'm sorry I lied."

* * *

When no one claimed it, Steven was able to wear his new Philadelphia pro hat to the banquet. As he sat around the table designated for the peewee *B* team he felt proud — proud of his team, his coach and of himself. They hadn't won the pennant, but they had lost only by one in the final game to North Van, their dreaded enemy. They had had a great year.

When it was their coach's turn he made a little speech and then presented Will with the trophy for the most outstanding player. Andrew won for the most dedicated and Steven nodded his approval as the whole hall clapped loudly.

Carter then went on to talk about a player who had shown great talent in both defence and offence, who had worked hard all year and who was a great asset to the team.

"Meatball, would you please come up and accept this trophy for the most improved and the best all-around player?"

Steven had never heard anything so sweet. A warm rush reddened his face as he moved through the crowded room. He glanced at the table where his dad was sitting and he saw the pride in his eyes. As he passed the bantam table, Jeff stood up and reached out.

"Way to go, bro," he said, slapping his hand.

* * *

Back home in his room, Steven hugged the trophy to his chest. He looked around for the perfect spot, a spot where everyone could see it. The shiny brass skater poised in a face-off was a prize like no other he had ever received. He kissed the plaque that held his name and placed it in the middle of his bookshelf.

"Yes!" he said as he stood back and admired. "Yes!"

Other books you'll enjoy in the Sports Stories series...

Baseball

☐ *Curve Ball* by John Danakas #1
Tom Poulos is looking forward to a summer of baseball in Toronto until his mother puts him on a plane to Winnipeg.

☐ *Baseball Crazy* by Martyn Godfrey #10
Rob Carter wins an all-expenses-paid chance to be batboy at the Blue Jays' spring training camp in Florida.

☐ *Shark Attack* by Judi Peers #25
The East City Sharks have a good chance of winning the county championship until their arch rivals get a tough new pitcher.

Basketball

☐ *Fast Break* by Michael Coldwell #8
Moving from Toronto to small-town Nova Scotia was rough, but when Jeff makes the school basketball team he thinks things are looking up.

☐ *Camp All-Star* by Michael Coldwell #12
In this insider's view of a basketball camp, Jeff Lang encounters some unexpected challenges.

☐ *Nothing but Net* by Michael Coldwell #18
The Cape Breton Grizzly Bears face an out-of-town basketball tournament they're sure to lose.

☐ *Slam Dunk* by Steven Barwin and Gabriel David Tick #23
In this sequel to *Roller Hockey Blues*, Mason Ashbury's basketball team adjusts to the arrival of some new players: girls.

Figure Skating

☐ *A Stroke of Luck* by Kathryn Ellis #6
Strange accidents are stalking one of the skaters at the Millwood Arena.

☐ *The Winning Edge* by Michele Martin Bosley #28
Jennie wants more than anything to win a grueling series of competitions, but is success worth losing her friends?

Gymnastics

☐ *The Perfect Gymnast* by Michele Martin Bossley #9
Abby's new friend has all the confidence she needs, but she also has a serious problem that nobody but Abby seems to know about.

Ice hockey

☐ *Shoot to Score* by Sandra Richmond #31
Playing defence on the B list, alongside the coach's mean-spirited son, are tough obstacles for Steven to overcome, but he perseveres and changes his luck.

☐ *Two Minutes for Roughing* by Joseph Romain #2
As a new player on a tough Toronto hockey team, Les must fight to fit in.

☐ *Hockey Night in Transcona* by John Danakas #7
Cody Powell gets promoted to the Transcona Sharks' first line, bumping out the coach's son who's not happy with the change.

☐ *Face Off* by C.A. Forsyth #13
A talented hockey player finds himself competing with his best friend for a spot on a select team.

☐ *Hat Trick* by Jacqueline Guest #20
The only girl on an all-boys' hockey team works to earn the captain's respect and her mother's approval.

☐ *Hockey Heroes* by John Danakas #22
A left-winger on the thirteen-year-old Transcona Sharks adjusts to a new best friend and his mom's boyfriend.

☐ *Hockey Heat Wave* by C.A. Forsyth #27
In this sequel to *Face Off*, Zack and Mitch encounter some trouble when it looks like only one of them will make the select team at hockey camp.

Riding

☐ *A Way With Horses* by Peter McPhee #11
A young Alberta rider invited to study show jumping at a posh local riding school uncovers a secret.

☐ *Riding Scared* by Marion Crook #15
A reluctant new rider struggles to overcome her fear of horses.

☐ *Katie's Midnight Ride* by C.A. Forsyth #16
An ambitious barrel racer finds herself without a horse weeks before her biggest rodeo.

☐ *Glory Ride* by Tamara L. Williams #21
Chloe Anderson fights memories of a tragic fall for a place on the Ontario Young Riders' Team.

☐ *Cutting it Close* by Marion Crook #24
In this novel about barrel racing, a talented young rider finds her horse is in trouble just as she is about to compete in an important event.

Roller hockey

☐ *Roller Hockey Blues* by Steven Barwin and Gabriel David Tick #17
Mason Ashbury faces a summer of boredom until he makes the roller-hockey team.

Running

☐ *Fast Finish* by Bill Swan #30
Noah is a promising young runner headed for the provincial finals when he suddenly decides to withdraw from the event.

Sailing

☐ *Sink or Swim* by William Pasnak #5
Dario can barely manage the dog paddle, but thanks to his mother he's spending the summer at a water sports camp.

Soccer

☐ *Lizzie's Soccer Showdown* by John Danakas #3
When Lizzie asks why the boys and girls can't play together, she
finds herself the new captain of the soccer team.

Swimming

☐ *Breathing Not Required* by Michele Martin Bossley #4
An eager synchronized swimmer works hard to be chosen for a
solo and almost loses her best friend in the process.

☐ *Water Fight!* by Michele Martin Bossley #14
Josie's perfect sister is driving her crazy but when she takes up
swimming — Josie's sport — it's too much to take.

☐ *Taking a Dive* by Michele Martin Bossley #19
Josie holds the provincial record for the butterfly, but in this
sequel to *Water Fight,* she can't seem to match her own time and
might not go on to the nationals.

☐ *Great Lengths* by Sandra Diersch #26
Fourteen-year-old Jessie decides to find out whether the ru-
mours about a new swimmer at her Vancouver club are true.

Track and Field

☐ *Mikayla's Victory* by Cynthia Bates #29
Mikayla must compete against her friend if she wants to repre-
sent her school at an important track event.